Edward Webster

Parliamentary Costs

SALZWASSER
VERLAG

Edward Webster

Parliamentary Costs

Reprint of the original, first published in 1864.

1st Edition 2022 | ISBN: 978-3-75259-451-5

Verlag (Publisher): Salzwasser Verlag GmbH, Zeilweg 44, 60439 Frankfurt, Deutschland
Vertretungsberechtigt (Authorized to represent): E. Roepke, Zeilweg 44, 60439 Frankfurt, Deutschland
Druck (Print): Books on Demand GmbH, In de Tarpen 42, 22848 Norderstedt, Deutschland

PARLIAMENTARY COSTS.

BY

EDWARD WEBSTER, ESQ

Second Edition.

LONDON

1864.

THE success which has attended the publication of the First Edition of the "Parliamentary Costs" has encouraged the publication of a Second Edition; every effort has been made to render this Edition as complete as possible, and it is confidently hoped that it will afford the fullest information upon the subject to which it relates.

The Author begs to record his thanks to those official and professional friends who have most courteously assisted him, in various ways, in the preparation of this Work.

TAXING OFFICE,
HOUSE OF COMMONS,
July, 1864.

CONTENTS.

INTRODUCTION.

PART I.

COSTS RELATIVE TO PRIVATE BILLS.

PART II.

COSTS RELATIVE TO THE TRIAL OF ELECTION PETITIONS.

PART III.

COSTS RELATIVE TO APPEAL CAUSES IN THE HOUSE OF LORDS.

PART I.

COSTS RELATIVE TO PRIVATE BILLS.

SECTION I.

TAXATION OF COSTS IN THE HOUSE OF COMMONS.

SECTION II.

BILLS OF COSTS, COUNSEL AND WITNESSES.

CHAPTER I.

CHAPTER II.

CHAPTER III.

SECTION III.

CHARGES SANCTIONED BY THE SPEAKER AND THE CLERK OF THE PARLIAMENT, IN ACCORDANCE WITH THE TAXATION ACTS.

SECTION IV.

SECTION V.

TAXATION ACTS.

PART II.

COSTS RELATIVE TO THE TRIAL OF ELECTION PETITIONS.

PART III.

COSTS RELATIVE TO APPEAL CAUSES IN THE HOUSE OF LORDS.

ERRATA.

Page 26, bottom line, *for* "at pp. 49, 50," *read* "at p. 52."

Page 29, line 6, *read* "Drawing Estimate."

Page 30, line 7, *after* "for the" *insert* "bill with agent's."

Page 32, line 12, *for* "observation" *read* "observations."

Pages 40 to 46, "Attending Mr. —— with brief," &c., *means in each instance a counsel.*

Page 44, line 14, *for the word* "and" *read* "&c."

Page 48, at bottom of the page, "Hotel," &c., *should stand*—

Hotel expenses	1	1	0
Fares, &c.	(sum paid)		

Page 61, line 12, *for* "reading" *read* "reaching."

Page 65, second line from bottom of the page, *should be* —

at per page of print	0	2	0
1*s. for each clerk.*			

Page 73, after line 7, *insert*—

Instructions for memorial as to non-compliance with Standing Orders .	0	13	4
Drawing memorial—			
If less than 11 folios	1	1	0
If more than 11 folios .. per folio	0	2	0

Page 75, line 19, *omit the word* "when."

Page 96, *the entry on Jan.* 12 *should be blanked out in the money column.*

INTRODUCTION.

The remuneration of the time and talents of one individual, employed for the benefit of another, generally varies with the nature of the services rendered, and although where that remuneration is defined by fixed prices for each specific thing done, it may be contended that the inefficient is paid at the same rate as the efficient practitioner, yet it must be remembered that the principle which rules all markets, namely, that the best talent is always in greatest demand, will secure to the man of ability such an excess of employment over his less-gifted neighbour as to compensate him for the wrong that he is so thought to sustain. Arbitrary scales.

It is evident that the more distinctly the principle and rate of charge is defined, and the better it is understood, the greater is the probability of justice being done to all; the honest man has nothing to fear by this publicity, and it remains for the man of doubtful probity to entertain fears, Extension of information as to costs.

the reason being that he first undertakes what his ignorance will not permit him to accomplish in a proper manner, and supplements this indiscretion by charging what usage forbids.

Principle involved in the consideration of costs.

The principle of costs is simply that of an equitable remuneration of one person employed in transacting business for another, and therefore when charges made by attornies excite unfavourable comment, it should be remembered that an attorney, unlike many other professional men, does not charge a single fee of large amount, but has to render a detailed account, and thus put together in small sums such an amount as is thought in the whole will justly remunerate him; these small sums or fees are the nearest ascertained value of each service rendered for them, and have been fixed by those whose duty it is to determine the value of such service, and consequently the client as well as the professional man have the benefit of their experience and impartiality.

Advisability of employing agents.

It is generally advisable for parties coming to Parliament to employ a parliamentary agent, as it secures the client's interests with more certainty and economy, and prevents a number of mistakes, which entail much expense on the client, and sometimes bring discredit to the solicitor. The solicitor does not, as very commonly is supposed, lose anything by the arrangement, as the charges made by the agent can never interfere with his own; neither are such charges in the character of agency fees. The parliamentary agent's familiarity with, and experience in, the passing of bills, secure the most useful and practicable legislative result to the client, and consequently credit to the solicitor. In oppositions, particularly, when every manœuvre permissible is frequently requisite to protect a client's interests, it is of the utmost importance that the more ready access to the authorities, familiarity with precedents and parliamentary information of the practised agent, should not be wanting.

PART I.

COSTS RELATIVE TO PRIVATE BILLS.

SECTION I.

TAXATION OF COSTS IN THE HOUSE OF COMMONS.

CHAPTER I.

APPLICATIONS FOR TAXATIONS.

THE Taxation Acts define costs relative to private bills as being "any costs, charges or expenses in respect of any proceedings" in Parliament "relating to any petition for a private bill, or private bill, or in respect of complying with the Standing Orders" of either House, "relative thereto, or in preparing, bringing in or carrying the same through, or in opposing the same," such costs being charged by "any attorney, solicitor, parliamentary agent or other person;" and the words "other person" has generally been held to apply only to a person filling the place of a solicitor or parliamentary agent, and not to an engineer, or to surveyors or persons of that class who may likewise be employed in the matter, although their bills have been taxed when they have been entered

Definition of parliamentary costs.

in bills of costs as disbursements, and their reasonableness has been challenged.

Careful perusal first necessary.

Before parties apply for a taxation they should try and satisfy themselves that it is worth while to have costs taxed, and whether the amount taken off is likely to exceed the costs and fees of taxation, as some experienced firms draw their bills out so well and moderately that the taxation only adds something to the bill instead of effecting a saving to the client.

Modes of application for taxations.

The application for a taxation may be made at the taxing office of the House of Commons, either in person and verbally, or by a letter addressed to the taxing officer, but the bill of costs should always be deposited in the taxing office at the same time that the application for its taxation is made; on the application being made the taxing officer appoints a day and hour for the taxation, the interval of time from the day of application to that appointed for the taxation being regulated according to the circumstances of the case; as for example, if the client or solicitor has to attend from Ireland or Scotland, a period of ten days is generally thought a reasonable interval; if from some place in England, a week, and sometimes less if in London. No written appointment is given by the taxing officer. The party applying for the taxation is required immediately to communicate the appointment to the other side, if any, or to his client if the taxation is purely an amicable one.

By whom application can be made.

Applications must be made either by the party liable to the costs or the solicitor or agent charging the costs; an individual member of a corporate body cannot make an application, unless the other members of such body delegate the office to him.

No application for a taxation can be entertained by the taxing officer if made by the client after a verdict shall have been obtained or a writ of inquiry executed in any action for the recovery of the costs. Neither can the taxing officer entertain an application for a taxation made by the client after the expiration of six months after the bill has been delivered, unless the solicitor charging the costs consents to such taxation; but if the client states special circumstances for such taxation taking place, the taxing officer can report them to the Speaker, who thereupon may direct the costs to be taxed; (these special circumstances should rather have reference to the causes which occasioned the delay in the application, than to the amount or character of the charges in the bill of costs.) When such an application is made by the client and resisted by the solicitor, the taxing officer would, if he felt disposed to think a taxation necessary, hear both parties before reporting the special circumstances to the Speaker.

Circumstances which prevent application being entertained.

Where a difficulty arises from the expiration of six months, or any other reason, in procuring the taxation of any bill in the ordinary manner, parties may procure a taxation by allowing the claimant to commence an action against them for the recovery of such costs, and then applying to the Court in which such action is brought to refer the costs to the taxing officer of the House of Commons, who then taxes such costs and returns

How these circumstances may be avoided.

them certified or accompanied by a separate certificate to such Court; or the Court may refer them to its own taxing officer, who can, under the 12th section of the Act 12 & 13 Vict. c. 78, request the taxing officer of the House of Commons to tax them.

CHAPTER II.

POWERS OF TAXING OFFICER.

THE powers conferred upon the taxing officer by the Taxation Acts (*a*), as to the actual process of taxation, may be briefly summed up as follows:— Powers of taxing officer on taxation.

By Clause 5 of both Acts he is empowered to examine parties and witnesses on oath, and may receive affidavits sworn before him or before any master in Chancery.

By Clause 6 he is empowered to call for the production of any books or writings in the hands of any party to the taxation relating to the matters of such taxation.

By Clause 10 of the Act 12 & 13 Vict. c. 78 (*b*), he may tax any costs not strictly taxable under the Act by which he exercises his authority, if comprised in a bill of costs, relative to a private bill, or he may request the proper officer of any Court to assist him in taxing any part of a bill.

And by Clause 13 of the last-mentioned Act he may take an account between the parties of all sums of money paid or received in respect of the bill of costs or any matters contained therein.

(*a*) See pp. 164 and 173, for these Acts.

(*b*) See p. 173, for this Act.

CHAPTER III.

PROCEDURE AT TAXATIONS.

Taxations. TAXATIONS may be either as between client and solicitor, or as between party and party.

Amicable taxation. In amicable cases sometimes the solicitor charging the costs only attends, and the client is not represented at all, in which cases, however, it is required of the solicitor that he produce a letter from his client, or some other evidence, that the client does not wish to be represented at the taxation. In these cases the taxing officer, having previously perused the bill, will require such explanations as he may think necessary with regard to any charges of irregular or unreasonable character, without going through the bill item by item with the solicitor.

In other amicable taxations the client is represented by a solicitor, who merely states that he is directed to attend on behalf of the client, who, however, has no wish to complain of the charges; in such cases as these such solicitor is generally understood to be present, for the purpose of furnishing authoritative explanations of such charges as the taxing officer may require fuller information upon, and he, in general, may be said to aid the taxation. He is also supposed to, what is commonly called, watch the taxation; and if any circumstance arises, such as the discovery of exorbitant or erroneous charges, or that the party charging the bill is supporting his charges in an irregular manner, he may then exercise the discretion of departing from his instructions, and act as if he were instructed to oppose the taxation.

In some instances parties on both sides consent to leave a bill with the taxing officer for his perusal without appearing, except to test the lengths of documents and vouch payments. If the taxing officer requires any explanations he requests the attendance of the party charging the bill. It is needless to add that this course is only practicable where the costs are strictly according to the scale.

In opposed cases a solicitor attends on behalf of the client to object to the charges made in the bill of costs. The taxing officer usually reads the charges in the bill seriatim, and the opposing solicitor objects to them as they are reached in this manner, or the taxing officer may not think it necessary to read each item, but may call upon the opposing solicitor to state at once the charges he objects to, and proceed to deal with the objections made in this manner. **Opposed taxations.**

These objections are usually, that the particular matter charged for was unnecessary,—that it was performed in so circuitous and roundabout a manner that the charges respecting it were unnecessarily multiplied,—that the amount of the charge exceeds that usually allowed by the taxing officer; and in the case of charges not usually incurred without specific instructions from the client that no such instructions had been given.

Charges omitted.

If it is discovered in the course of taxation that any charges have been omitted, they are allowed to be inserted in the bill.

Settling.

At the conclusion of the taxation the lengths of all documents are tested, and vouchers are produced for all disbursements charged in the bill; it is absolutely necessary that every disbursement (*a*) should be vouched before the taxing officer certifies or reports the amount allowed by him. The costs and fees of taxation are also then settled, and the taxing officer exercises the power given to him by the Act (*b*), and awards the costs, and charges the fees of taxation as he thinks fit, having regard to the manner in which the bill has been drawn up and the amount taxed off it (*c*).

Costs of taxation.

Taxing officer's report.

When the taxation is concluded and all the disbursements vouched, as already stated, the taxing officer reports (*d*) the result of the taxation to the Speaker; this report is filed in the taxing office, and a signed duplicate is at once given to the party entitled to it, namely, the party who in the first instance applied for the taxation; it sometimes happens, however, that parties desire to

(*a*) The reasonableness of disbursements can always be challenged, and submitted to the taxing officer to be dealt with by him.

(*b*) See p. 168, s. 7 of Act.

(*c*) If more than a sixth is taxed off the bill, the party charging the bill has to pay the fees of the taxation, and also the costs of taxation, of the other side.

(*d*) See p. 158, for form of this document.

have the Speaker's certificate (*a*) of the taxation, or they desire to complain of the taxation, for the latter purpose a period of twenty-one days is allowed, within which the parties may deposit in the taxing office a memorial (*b*) setting forth the grounds of their complaint, such memorial is subsequently endorsed by the Speaker, if he thinks fit, with a direction to the taxing officer to make a further report with regard to the matters complained of, and upon this further report being made the Speaker decides whether there are grounds for varying the taxing officer's report of the taxation; upon the matter being so disposed of, or if no memorial has been so deposited, then, at the expiration of the twenty-one days the parties may, if they so desire, have the Speaker's certificate. The occasions when the Speaker's certificate is demanded are exceedingly rare, being limited mostly to the cases where an action has been commenced, or intended to be commenced, for the recovery of the costs, the certificate having the authority of a warrant to confess judgment.

Speaker's certificate.

Memorial against taxing officer's taxation.

Parties are mostly content to accept the duplicate of the taxing officer's report as a sufficient evidence of the result of the taxation.

(*a*) See p. 159, for form of this document.

(*b*) See p. 160.

CHAPTER IV.

MISCELLANEOUS TAXATIONS.

References from taxing masters of Courts of law and equity.

THERE is a class of taxations of not very common occurrence, respecting which it seems advisable to say a few words. By Clause 12 of the Act 12 & 13 Vict. c. 78, "the proper officer of any other Court" may request the taxing officer "to assist him in taxing and settling any costs, charges and expenses incurred in respect of a private bill, being part of any bill of costs which shall have been referred to him by the Court of which he is such officer;" and the taxing officer may "thereupon proceed to tax and settle the same and return the same with his opinion thereupon" to such officer. In these cases the costs in question are generally endorsed by the taxing master or officer of the Court of law, with a request to the taxing officer of the House of Commons to tax them, who on receiving the costs gives an appointment and proceeds with the taxation in the same manner as already described, and when it is concluded endorses a certificate (*a*) on the bill of costs, and delivers it to the party who applied for the taxation.

References from Judges.

The Judges of the several Courts in England, Ireland and Scotland, have at different times referred costs to the taxing officer of the House of Commons to tax the same both as to the amount

(*a*) See p. 161, for form of this certificate.

properly chargeable, and in cases of disputed agreements to define what are the costs within the terms of the agreement, or strictly necessary and incidental to the proceedings in Parliament. In these cases the taxing officer, on receipt of the order of reference together with the costs, appoints a day and proceeds with the taxation in the manner already described, and on the termination of the taxation grants a certificate (*a*) of his taxation, and returns the bill of costs to the party who applied for the taxation.

As to certain costs in the case of Ireland.

By the 6th section of 16 & 17 Vict. c. 136, (Public Works Acts Amendment (Ireland) Bill,) the actual "bill duly taxed and certified by the taxing officer" must be laid before grand juries in Ireland, before any presentment in respect thereof can be made, and it is therefore the practice of the taxing officer, after taxing the costs in the usual manner, to endorse a certificate on the bill which he taxes, and return the bill to the parties for the purpose of being so laid before the grand jury.

Witnesses' costs.

Exorbitant charges made by witnesses can be taxed if they are put in the form of disbursements into any solicitor or agents' bill, which is submitted to the taxing officer. If it is desirable to tax this description of costs and not the solicitor's own bill, the solicitor can make out a bill-heading in his own name against the client, and put such charges as are so desired to be taxed, as disbursements in such bill, and apply for its taxation in the usual manner.

(*a*) See p. 162, for form of these certificates.

CHAPTER V.

PROTESTS, AND LOCUS STANDI OF PARTIES.

Protests. When liability denied. WHEN a client denies his liability to the payment of costs, but yet is not desirous of finding, after a Court of law adjudges him liable, that he has lost the benefit of opposing the taxation, he can, by his solicitor, or himself, attend and oppose the taxation under protest, that his attendance thereat is not to be taken as an admission of his liability.

When jurisdiction of taxing officer denied. And, in the same manner, if a solicitor disputes the jurisdiction of the taxing officer, or the right of the client to tax his costs, he can still attend the taxation under protest that his doing so is not to be taken as a recognition of such jurisdiction or an admission of such right.

Locus standi of parties at taxations. If the client is a company, corporation, trustees or any other body made up of different persons, individual members of such bodies have no right of their own accord to attend, or delegate others to attend, and oppose a taxation, it being assumed that the client will, if they think necessary, instruct and duly authorize some person to discharge this duty.

In the case of certain bodies not possessing the character of clients, yet having eventually to pay costs, such as vestries liable to the payment of costs incurred by the Metropolitan Board of Works in passing any act, representatives of such bodies have no such *locus standi* before the taxing officer as will enable them to attend and oppose a taxation; there is nothing, however, to prevent their being present during the taxation (*a*).

The taxation of the taxing officer has no effect on the question of liability to payment of costs taxed by him, that is a question entirely for a Court of law, and his decision only extends to the propriety of the charges made. **Taxing officer has no jurisdiction as to question of liability.**

It has been ruled that the parliamentary agent is employed by the solicitor, and that supposing a company to promote or oppose any bill in Parliament, they employ the solicitor, and are liable to him only and not to the parliamentary agent (*b*). **Solicitor liable to parliamentary agent.**

(*a*) So decided by Mr. Lefroy in the case of the Metropolis Gas Regulation Act costs in 1861.

(*b*) So ruled by Sir Walter Riddell, on a reference to his arbitration from the Court of Exchequer, in the case of *Dorington* v. *Maltby*, in 1849.

SECTION II.

BILLS OF COSTS—COUNSEL AND WITNESSES.

CHAPTER I.

BILLS OF COSTS.

The following Bills of Costs have been made out by the author according to the authorized Scale, which will be found at p. 124.

REMARKS.

Course of bill as assumed in these bills of costs. It is assumed that the following bills commence in the House of Commons, in the case therefore of bills commencing in the House of Lords, although the proceedings would be identical up to the stage where they go before the examiner, after that it would be necessary to turn to the first stage in the Lords, and return subsequently to the first stage in the Commons.

Plan of bills. The following are merely the outlines of bills of costs; many attendances and other charges occur during the progress of a bill which are not set out here, the course of bills differing too much to make such an attempt of any practical utility; the solicitor or agent must follow the narrative of his own diary, and supply the omission.

The bills are adapted to opposed Second Class Bills (except that at p. 92,) so as to exhaust, as far as practicable, all the charges in the scale; discretion, therefore, must be exercised in selecting the charges, no charge being allowed on taxation except for work actually done.

Where charges are blanked out, it signifies that they are covered by the sessional fee, for which, see p. 136.

The expression "attending you" throughout these bills means the client, or, if a company, the secretary.

The copies stated throughout the bills are the number allowed to be charged, and at the rate stated; if in any special case further copies should be required, 4*d*. a folio is the rate at which they must be charged. **Copies.**

The charges given for attornies or solicitors are allowed in common to attornies or solicitors in England and Ireland, and to writers to the signet in Scotland.

Parliamentary agents in London doing Scotch business are allowed to make out their bills of costs on the Attorney or Solicitor's Scale, and not on that for Parliamentary Agents. **Parliamentary agents.**

It is generally advisable to place disbursements in a separate column, or at the end of the bill. **Disbursements.**

A solicitor filling any office to which a salary is attached, such as vestry clerk, clerk to road trustees, or to a corporation, &c., and being instructed by them to promote or oppose a bill in parliament, must be careful not to charge for **Solicitors holding offices.**

those things which his salary would properly cover.

Charges other than parliamentary. Any charges included in a bill of costs for proceedings previously to those connected with the preparation of the bill, or the notice or plans for the same, or for other proceedings which are not strictly parliamentary, must be made out according to the scale allowed in Courts of law.

Drawing. In all cases the charge for drawing any document includes the fair copy to keep, or for counsel or agent to settle. No further charge is therefore allowed for any of those purposes.

Printed documents. Where copies are allowed, prints may be charged as copies, except where specially mentioned in the scale of charges, but otherwise only expense of printing.

Minutes of evidence. On the 16th February, 1864, the House of Commons resolved, "That the minutes of evidence on opposed private bills be printed at the expense of the parties whenever copies of the same be required." Manuscript copies of evidence before Commons' committee cannot be charged, but the printer's bill only.

AN ATTORNEY'S OR SOLICITOR'S BILL OF COSTS *for promoting a Private Bill.*

In Parliament,
SESSION 1864.

THE ——— COMPANY, DR.

To MESSRS. ———, of ———,
Solicitors,

In respect of promoting, in Parliament, on behalf of the said Company, the ——— Act, 1864.

Where throughout the Scale distinct charges are assigned to the Solicitor and to the Parliamentary Agent for the same service, but which service can be only charged for by the person who performed it, and therefore, for the most part, cannot be charged by the Solicitor unless he is acting as Parliamentary Agent, such charges are stated in this Bill of Costs.

THE following charges should be made for general attendances and time :—

The charges for attendances throughout should be:—

	£	s.	d.
Ordinary	0	6	8
		to	
	0	13	4
If upwards of an hour ..	1	1	0
Or, per hour	0	13	4
If required to leave London:			
Time, per day	4	4	0
Hotel expenses ..	1	1	0
Fares, &c.	(sum paid)		

		£	s.	d.
	Attending members or peers at the Houses on special and necessary occasions (other than moving the stages of the bill)	1	1	0
	If a clerk:			
	Attendances	0	6	8
	Time, per day	1 to 2	1 to 2	0 to 0
	[*Generally charged* ..	1	11	6]
	See also attendances, &c., covered by sessional fee, at p. 139.			
	The charges for letters are—			
	Ordinary	0	3	6
	Containing professional advice or instructions	0	5	0
	If exceeding six folios	0	10	0

		£	s.	d.
Oct. 28.	Instructions for notice in Gazette and newspapers	0	13	4
	Drawing notice—			
	If less than eleven folios	1	1	0
	If more than eleven folios, per folio ..	0	2	0
	Attending parliamentary agents therewith to settle, and instructing them	0	13	4
	(If attendance actually had.)			
	Letter to parliamentary agent with notice	0	5	0

		£ s. d.
Nov. 7.	Having received draft notice as settled by parliamentary agents, fair copy thereof for Messrs. ——, in the country, at per folio	0 0 4
	Letter therewith	0 5 0
„ 10.	Copies of notice, as finally settled, for insertion in the newspapers and Gazette, at per folio	0 0 6
	Forwarding same to editor and instructing him .. .. .. or Attending at office of newspaper, instructing	0 6 8
	On receipt of proof, examining same	0 3 4 to 0 10 0
	Returning proof and ordering insertion for three weeks	0 6 8
	If a revise is necessary, an addition for ordering revise and examining same, of each revise	0 10 0
	No other or further charge is allowed with reference to printing the notice. *The foregoing charges apply to each newspaper.* *No charge is allowed for copies of the notice for deposit with the plans, &c., printer's slips being so deposited; nor are any charges allowed for copies of notice after it is printed.*	
„ 12.	Having received the —— newspaper with first publication of notice, examining same	0 3 4

		£	s.	d.
Nov. 13.	Clerks engaged on the ground taking reference, each clerk, at per day.. For time	1	11	6
	Hotel expenses, and fares	(sum paid)		
	If a managing clerk is necessary to superintend the referencing he is charged at—			
	Time, per day ..	2	2	0
	Hotel expenses, and fares	(sum paid)		
„ 14.	Writing to different persons as to their interest in properties, each letter	0	5	0
„ 20.	Drawing book of reference, at per folio	0	2	0
	Copies thereof for deposit, as required by the Standing Orders, at per folio	0	0	9
	One copy only is allowed, for the deposit of portions thereof, amongst parish officers.			
	Copy for marking section for applications to owners, &c., at per folio..	0	0	6
	Copy for use of engineer or other professional person engaged in the case, if positively requisite, at per folio	0	0	4
	Although the book of reference is frequently printed, the copies before stated are allowed as copies, but			

		£ s. d.
	the printer's bill must not be charged, nor any further copies, except under special circumstances.	
Nov. 21.	Having received the —— newspaper with second publication of notice, examining same	0 3 4
„ 28.	Examining and making up plans and books of reference for the purpose of deposit, each set	0 10 6
	The examining and making up the deposits for the parish clerks to be charged according to the time occupied, at per hour	0 13 4
	[If solicitor is acting as parliamentary agent he may charge:	
	Attending at the Private Bill Office (Commons) to deposit plan, section and book of reference	1 1 0
	The like at Parliament Office ..	1 1 0
	The like at Board of Trade or Admiralty	0 13 4]
	Instructions for bill	2 2 0
	Drawing bill, at per folio	0 2 0
	Additional clauses are allowed at the same rate.	
	Having received the —— newspaper with third publication of notice, examining same	0 3 4

		£ s. d.
Nov. 30.	Attending at offices of clerks of the peace to deposit plan, &c., and on parish clerks to deposit portions thereof, each attendance ..	0 13 4

If at a distance, and for deposits with parish clerks, &c. (if numerous), clerk's time and expenses are to be charged instead of the preceding.

The charge for attending to deposit includes any charge for drawing a memorandum of documents deposited, and obtaining signature of the depositor thereto, and the requisite copies of the same, except the same shall exceed one folio, when 1s. 4d. per folio may be charged for drawing the same, and 6d. per folio for copies to hand in to examiner or other requisite copies; it also includes the drawing and obtaining the certificate or receipt for such deposit.

Attendances for the purpose of deposit cannot be charged both by parliamentary agent and solicitor.

The solicitor generally makes the deposits with the clerk of the peace and the parish clerks, and the parliamentary agent with the Houses of Parliament and Government Offices.

No charge is allowed for copies of Gazette notice for deposit, printer's slips being deposited.

	Forwarding bill to parliamentary agent to settle	— — —

Conferences with the parliamentary agent on the bill will probably arise and alterations be made; these will be charged at the attendance rate, and alterations at the drawing rate; the parliamentary agent superintends the printing of the bill; but if solicitor is acting as parliamentary agent he will find charges relative to printing at pp. 49, 50.

		£	s.	d.
Dec. 7.	Drawing index to book of reference and register therewith, for preparing applications and for entering up service thereof, with answers received (including necessary copies), per folio ..	0	1	4
	The entering the replies received from time to time is covered by this charge, and that for drawing the lists of owners, &c., for deposit.			
	Drawing a fair copy for service, applications or notices to owners, lessees and occupiers of property, with schedules thereto and letter of assent, dissent or neutrality to accompany same, at each notice ..	0	10	0
	Notices other than in the form set forth in Appendix A. of the Standing Orders, such as of relinquishment,—to millowners,—in case of burial grounds, &c.,—of crown, &c., property and of repeal of statutory provisions, are allowed at			
	per notice	0	5	0
	Drawing list of applications to be posted or to be served by a witness, and copy for signature, including the obtaining the signature of the witness thereto:			
	Each list	0	3	4
	or, per folio	0	1	4
	No second charge allowed for drawing the above lists of applications for the purpose of handing into the examiner, or other purpose, but only the charge for copying.			

		£	s.	d.
Dec. 7.	Attending posting applications and taking postmaster's receipt ..	0	13	4
	This method of service should always be adopted, if practicable and most economical. *If personal service is required or a journey is made to a post town, clerk's time and expenses may be charged at 1l. 11s. 6d. for time; and hotel expenses and fares, as paid, except where such service can be made more economically through local agents.* *A separate charge for service of each notice is not allowed, except under special circumstances.*			
„ 16.	Drawing petition for leave to bring in bill—			
	If less that eleven folios ..	1	1	0
	If more, per folio	0	2	0
	Attending parliamentary agent therewith to settle, and instructing him	0	13	4
„ 18.	Having received petition for bill back from parliamentary agent settled, ingrossing same, per folio ..	0	0	9
	Letter to Mr. —— for appointment to sign petition [*or* to fix seal of company]	0	5	0
„ 19.	Attending Mr. ——, procuring his signature to petition for bill [*or* affixing seal]	0	13	4
	Letter to parliamentary agent with petition	—	—	—
„ 21.	Attending engineer, conferring on estimate and other matters ..	0	13	4

		£	s.	d.
Dec. 21.	Drawing lists of owners, lessees and occupiers, per folio	0	2	0
	Two copies for deposit in Parliament Office and Private Bill Office, per folio	0	0	9
	Estimate of expense and requisite copies	0	10	6
	[*or*, Declaration in lieu or in aid of deposit of money, and requisite copies	1	1	0
	Declaration and estimate, and requisite copies	1	11	6
	Declaration under Standing Order 41, as to capital, shares, &c., and requisite copies	1	1	0
	Subscription contract—			
	Instructions	0	13	4
	Per folio	0	1	4]
	Attending Mr. ——, obtaining his signature [to any of these documents]	0	6	8
	Forwarding these documents to parliamentary agent for deposit ..	—	—	—
	Or, if acting as parliamentary agent, making up same 10s. 6d., and depositing same 10s. 6d. for Private Bill Office, 10s. 6d. for Parliament Office, and 10s. 6d. for depositing prints in Vote Office.			
„ 23.	[If solicitor is acting as parliamentary agent he may charge—			

		£	s.	d.
Dec. 23.	Drawing agent's declaration, and copies for deposit:			
	1st class bill	1	1	0
	2nd class bill	2	2	0
	Attending at the Private Bill Office (Commons) to deposit the petition for the declaration and printed copy of the bill annexed, and other printed copies of the bill, and registering the petition in the general list of petitions	1	1	0]
	The making up the petition, with declaration and bill annexed, is included in the above charge.			
„ 28.	Drawing requisition to clerk in Private Bill Office for his warrant for payment of parliamentary deposit ..	0	10	0
	This charge includes copy for signature.			
1864. Jan. 5.	The parliamentary agent having returned the requisition for warrant to receive deposit, attending different promoters for their signatures thereto .. each	0	6	8
	Attending the engineer, discussing various matters, and particularly opposition of Mr. ——	0	13	4
„ 6.	Letter to engineer requesting him to meet Mr. ——	0	3	6
	Preparing circulars convening meeting of directors, each	0	1	0

		£	s.	d.
Jan. 8.	Attending meeting of directors relative to obtaining money for the deposit, upwards of an hour ..	1	1	0
	Charges incidental to borrowing money for the deposit are not allowed on a taxation, such practice being considered as in contravention to the intention of parliament in requiring this guarantee.			
	Drawing warrant for payment of parliamentary deposit	0	10	0
	This includes copy for signature.			
	Drawing affidavit verifying signature to warrant	0	10	0
	Letter to parliamentary agent therewith, and as to money to be deposited	0	5	0
„ 11.	Having received warrant, signed, from parliamentary agent, attending at accountant general's to deposit same and bespeak directions ..	0	13	4
„ 12.	Attending for and obtaining his directions for payment of money into Court, and subsequently attending broker and making arrangement for transfer	0	13	4
„ 14.	Attending in city and at Bank of England, with parties, making transfer. Engaged two hours ..	1	6	8
„ 16.	Attending bespeaking certificate of amount paid into Court, and afterwards for same	0	13	4
	The last four charges can only be			

		£	s.	d.
	made by the person who actually acted: if the parliamentary agent did, then the solicitor must not charge, and vice versâ.			
Jan. 16.	Having received copy of a memorial against this bill on Standing Orders, perusing same:			
	If under twenty folios..	0	6	8
	If above, per folio ..	0	0	4
	Attendance upon you, conferring thereon	0	13	4
	Drawing observation on memorial for parliamentary agent, per folio ..	0	1	4
	Attending him thereon, upwards of an hour	1	1	0
	Copy memorial, for use before examiner, at per folio	0	0	6
	Copy memorial, for use of engineer [if necessary], at per folio	0	0	6
	Drawing [*or* if already drawn by parliamentary agent, perusing and filling up] statement of proofs for examiner for Standing Orders, and arranging documents referred to therein, and forwarding same to parliamentary agent:			
	1st class bill..	1	1	0
	Ditto, where lands and houses are taken	2	2	0
	2nd class bill	3	3	0

		£	s.	d.
Jan. 16.	[If the solicitor is also acting as parliamentary agent, he may charge for drawing statement of proofs, including final arrangement of the same:			
	1st class bill..	2	2	0
	Ditto, when lands and houses are taken	3	3	0
	2nd class bill	4	4	0]
„ 19.	Drawing affidavit by Mr. ——, as to applications to owners, &c., served by him	0	10	0
	Or per folio	0	1	4
	This includes instructions or attendance on witness, list of owners, &c. attached, and copy.			
	Attending, swearing same [*or* attending with witness to be sworn] ..	0	6	8
	These charges are repeated for each affidavit.			
	Two copies of lists of applications served by Mr. ——, a witness, for use before the examiner, at per folio	0	0	6
	This charge is repeated for each such witness.			
„ 26.	Attending engineer, reading over proofs and arranging for his attendance before examiner	0	6	8
„ 27.	One copy statement of proofs for own use before examiner, at per folio..	0	0	6
	The other copies are charged by the parliamentary agent.			
„ 28.	Attending before examiner, petition in the list, but not called on ..	2	2	0

		£	s.	d.
Jan. 29.	Attending before examiner to prove compliance with Standing Orders; memorial of ——, inquired into, and examiner decided that Standing Orders had not been complied with..	from 3	3	0
		to 5	5	0
	[If the petition is unopposed the attendance before the examiner will be—			
	In 1st class bills	2	2	0
	In 2nd class bills	3	3	0
	or, If a petition is adjourned for further proofs, each subsequent attendance when the examiner shall inquire into the same, or attending to apply for postponement or adjournment	1	1	0]
	When two or more petitions for bills, being promoted or opposed by or on behalf of the same clients, are appointed for consideration by the same examiner on the same day, but are not called on, the solicitors of such clients will not be entitled to such charge in respect of each petition for a bill so promoted or opposed, but may charge any sum not exceeding 1l. 1s. for additional trouble (if any) in respect of each other petition for a bill on the same list; provided that in no case (except under special circumstances) shall a charge exceeding 5l. 5s. be made in respect of one such day's attendance on behalf of the same clients.			
	Attendance of clerk to give evidence	0	10	6
	And same for each clerk giving evidence.			
	[If in favour of or against an opposed bill, or against allegations of a memorial	1	1	0]

		£ s. d.
	Only the single attendance is allowed to be charged for proofs before the examiner in respect of the Standing Orders of both Houses, when the same are taken simultaneously.	
Feb. 5.	Attending parliamentary agent with names of members who had consented to bring in bill	0 6 8
	Attending House of Commons on presentation of petition for bill ..	1 1 0
	The attendance at the House, on the member who presents the petition, is included in this charge. *When the solicitor is also acting as parliamentary agent, he will be entitled to charge 2l. 2s. for his attendance at the House on this stage of the bill.*	
	Attending meeting of Lord Chairman, and Chairman of Ways and Means as to which House the several bills should commence in, when it was decided that this bill should commence in the Commons ..	1 1 0
" 9.	Perusing and considering examiner's report, as to non-compliance ..	0 6 8
" 11.	Drawing statement for Standing Orders Committee (Commons), stating circumstances in favour of dispensing with Standing Orders and forwarding same to parliamentary agent to settle	from 0 13 4 to 2 0 0
" 12.	Attending Standing Orders Committee, when they resolved on reporting in favour of dispensing with the Standing Orders ..	2 2 0

		£	s.	d.
Feb. 15.	Attending House of Commons when bill read first time	1	1	0
	This includes attending the member at the House who makes the motion.			
" 22.	Attending House when bill read second time	1	1	0
	This includes attending the member at the House who makes the motion. When the solicitor is also acting as parliamentary agent, he will be entitled to charge 2l. 2s. for his attendance at the House on this stage of the bill.			
	Perusing and considering Lord Chairman's remarks on the bill ..	0 1	10 to 1	6 0
" 23.	Perusing copy petition of Mr. —— against the bill—			
	If under twenty folios ..	0	6	8
	If above, per folio ..	0	0	4
	And same charge for each petition against.			
	Attending you as to Lord Chairman's remarks on bill	0	13	4
" 24.	Attending Chairman of Ways and Means, who had desired to see us with reference to certain clauses in this bill (if required to accompany parliamentary agent) ..	1	1	0
	Drawing and copy retainer to Mr. ——	0	10	0
	Attending him therewith	0	10	0
	Paid his fee and clerk	(sum paid)		
	These charges should be repeated for each counsel.			

		£ s. d.
Feb. 25.	Drawing statement for Standing Orders Committee (Lords), in favour of dispensing with Standing Orders	from 0 13 4 to 2 0 0
	Or per sheet of ten folios..	0 13 4
„ 26.	Attending Standing Orders Committee (Lords), when they resolved on reporting in favour of dispensing with the Standing Orders ..	2 2 0
„ 27.	Attending committee of selection [*or* committee on railway and canal bills] on nomination of committee and arrangement of groups ..	from 1 1 0 to 2 2 0
„ 28.	Attending Mr. Speaker's counsel to go through bill	1 1 0
	This is charged by the solicitor, only when he is acting as parliamentary agent; or if he is specially required to accompany the parliamentary agent. *Subsequent attendances are* 13*s.* 4*d.*	
March 1.	Drawing petition in favour of bill—	
	If less than eleven folios	0 13 4
	If less than fifteen folios	1 0 0
	If more than fifteen folios, per sheet	0 13 4
	or, per folio	0 1 4
	And so on for each petition in favour. *No charge is allowed for instructions for petition, or for endorsing and making up same.*	
	Forwarding same to parliamentary agent	— — —

		£	s.	d.
March 3.	Letter therewith to Messrs. —— at ——, instructing them to obtain signatures thereto	0	5	0

		£	s.	d.
	If there is a petition for additional provision, the following are the charges:			
	Instructions for clauses proposed to be inserted on petition for additional provision	0	13	4
	Drawing same .. per folio	0	2	0
	Drawing petition for additional provision—			
	If less than eleven folios..	1	1	0
	If more than eleven folios, per folio	0	2	0
	Forwarding same to parliamentary agent	—	—	—
„ 4.	Having received clauses printed, and petition settled, engrossing petition .. .. at per folio	0	0	9
	Procuring signature thereto	0	13	4
	If notices are published and plans, &c. are deposited, the charges are the same as for complying with the Standing Orders in those particulars previously to introduction of bill.			
	Drawing [*or* perusing] statement of proofs, and arranging papers, &c.	from 1	1	0
		to 2	2	0

		£	s.	d.
March 4.	Forwarding these documents to agent	—	—	—
„ 7.	Attending examiner, same inquired into—			
	If unopposed.. .	1	1	0
	If opposed ..	2	2	0
			to	
		3	0	0
	If necessary to go before the Standing Orders Committee, the charges are the same as on the petition for the bill.			

	£	s.	d.
[If solicitor is acting as parliamentary agent:—Attending at the Private Bill Office to deposit petitions in favour of bill, and registering the same; viz.:—			
If one petition, or less than three	0	13	4
If three petitions, and less than seven	1	1	0
If seven petitions, and less than twelve	1	11	6
For any number exceeding twelve	2	2	0
These charges cover the endorsing petitions and preparing the same for deposit; but if forwarded by the solicitor to parliamentary agent for deposit, from 3s. 4d. to 6s. 8d. is allowed for endorsing a petition or set of petitions, and transmitting the same to the agent for the purpose of deposit.]			

		£ s. d.
March 12.	Instructions for brief in the House of Commons (according to circumstances).	
	Drawing brief, per sheet of ten folios	0 13 4
	Where documents, such as tables, petitions, &c., being already drawn, form part of the brief, they are only allowed in this charge for drawing the brief as copy, at 6d. a folio.	
	Copies of brief for counsel; not exceeding three .. at per folio	0 0 6
	Copies of petitions against, for use of counsel; not exceeding three copies .. at per folio	0 0 6
	Instructions for proof of Mr. ——, including attendance on the witness to take notes of his evidence ..	0 13 4
	Drawing proofs, per sheet of ten folios	0 13 4
	Attending Mr. ——, settling his proof (if necessary)	0 6 8
	Copies thereof for counsel; not exceeding three, at per folio	0 0 6
	And so on for all the proofs. *If it becomes necessary to draw further proofs, they are allowed at the same rates.* *Drawing statements, abstracts, &c., and copies of other documents required in committee, are allowed at those rates.*	
„ 14.	Attending Mr. —— with brief and papers and to pay fee	0 10 0
	Paid his fee and clerk	(sum paid)
	The like attendance on Mr. —— ..	0 10 0
	Paid his fee and clerk	(sum paid)

		£ s. d.
March 15.	Attending Mr. —— (*a counsel*) to appoint consultation	0 10 0
	Paid his fee and clerk	(sum paid)
	The like attendance on Mr. —— ..	0 10 0
	Paid his fee and clerk	(sum paid)
	Attending parliamentary agent, informing him of consultation	— — —
„ 16.	Attending consultation, discussing and considering evidence, &c., &c. ..	1 1 0
	Attending all day, watching committee on this group, but the bill was not reached	2 2 0
	Attending Mr. —— (*a counsel*) bespeaking his attendance in committee to-morrow	0 10 0
	Paid his fee and clerk	(sum paid)
	The like attendance on Mr. —— ..	0 10 0
	Paid his fee and clerk	(sum paid)
„ 17.	Attending committee, case opened and partly proceeded with .. .. *This charge is allowed with or without counsel, and on consideration of preamble or clauses.*	3 3 0 to 5 5 0
	Attending Mr. —— (*a counsel*) appointing consultation for the morning	0 10 0
	Paid his fee and clerk	(sum paid)
	The like attendance on Mr. —— ..	0 10 0
	Paid his fee and clerk	(sum paid)

		£ s. d.
March 18.	Attending consultation	1 1 0
	Attending Mr. —— (*a counsel*) with minutes of evidence, &c., bespeaking his attendance in committee	0 10 0
	Paid his fee and clerk	(sum paid)
	The like attendance on Mr. —— ..	0 10 0
	Paid his fee and clerk	(sum paid)
	Attending committee all day, witnesses examined, &c.	3 3 0 to 5 5 0

It will be seen from the foregoing what the charges incidental to counsel and the committee are, and they will have to be repeated for each day the bill is considered by the committee; other attendances and matters may arise which must be charged at the rates given in the scale.

When two or more bills, being promoted by or on behalf of the same clients, are appointed for consideration by the committee on the same day, but are postponed or adjourned without being considered, or are not separately considered by the committee, the solicitors of such clients respectively will not be entitled to such charge in respect of each bill, so promoted or opposed; but may charge any sum not exceeding 1l. 1s. for additional trouble (if any) in respect of each other bill so postponed or adjourned, or not separately considered; provided that in no case (except under special circumstances) shall a charge exceeding 5l. 5s. be made in respect of one such day's attendance upon the committee on behalf of the same clients.

		£ s. d.
	No charge is allowed for attendance of a clerk to the solicitor on a committee, except for the purpose of being examined as a witness. *See page 20, for remarks as to minutes of evidence.*	
Mar. 18.	[But if the bill were unopposed the following would be the charges in respect of the committee:	
	Attending when the bill was considered by the committee ..	3 3 0
	Under special circumstances in railway and other bills	from 3 3 0 to 5 5 0]
	Attending the committee to apply for a postponement or adjournment ..	1 1 0
Apr. 25.	Attending House on consideration of report	1 1 0
	When the solicitor is also acting as parliamentary agent, he will be entitled to charge 2l. 2s. for his attendance at the House on this stage of the bill.	
„ 27.	Attending House of Commons on bill being read third time and passed	1 1 0
	When the solicitor is also acting as parliamentary agent, he will be entitled to charge 2l. 2s. for his attendance at the House on this stage of the bill.	
	Attending House of Lords on bill being read first time and referred to the examiners	1 1 0
„ 28.	Drawing and copy retainer to Mr. ——	0 10 0

		£	s.	d.
Apr. 28.	Attending him therewith and with fee	0	10	0
	Paid his fee and clerk	(sum paid)		
	And so on for each counsel.			
May 3.	Drawing statement of proofs for examiner as to compliance with Standing Orders not previously inquired into; and arranging and putting up documents referred to therein	from 1 to 2	1 to 2	0 to 0
	If the solicitor is acting as parliamentary agent, instead of preceding	from 2 to 3	2 to 3	0 to 3
	The charges for affidavits, copies of memorials, and if required, are the same as on introduction of bill.			
	Forwarding same to parliamentary agent	—	—	—
„ 4.	Attending examiner, further proofs given and Standing Orders found complied with:—			
	If unopposed	1	1	0
	If opposed	2 to 3	2 to 3	0 to 0
	Clerk attending as witness	0	10	6

If no further Standing Orders are applicable, it is not necessary for the solicitor to attend, as this is done by the agent.

If the Standing Orders are found not to have been complied with, the charges incidental to the Standing Orders Committee will be the same as at the introduction of the bill, which see.

		£ s. d.
May 6.	Perusing copy, petition of ——, against the bill:—	
	If under twenty folios..	0 6 8
	If above, per folio ..	0 0 4
	And same charge for each petition against.	
„ 9.	Instructions for brief	— — —
	For the charges relative to the brief, proofs, &c., see p. 40.	
„ 10.	Attending Mr. ——, with brief and papers and to pay fee	0 10 0
	Paid his fee and clerk..	(sum paid)
	The like attendance on Mr. —— ..	0 10 0
	Paid his fee and clerk..	(sum paid)
„ 11.	Attending Mr. —— (*a counsel*), to appoint consultation	0 10 0
	Paid his fee and clerk..	(sum paid)
	The like attendance on Mr. —— ..	0 10 0
	Paid his fee and clerk..	(sum paid)
	Attending House of Lords when bill read a second time, and a committee was appointed who fixed their first sitting for the 13th ..	1 1 0
	If solicitor acts as parliamentary agent he can charge 2l. 2s. for his attendance.	
„ 12.	Attending consultation	1 1 0
	Attending Mr. —— (*a counsel*), bespeaking his attendance in committee to-morrow..	0 10 0
	Paid his fee and clerk..	(sum paid)

		£ s. d.
May 12.	The like attendance on Mr. —— ..	0 10 0
	Paid his fee and clerk..	(sum paid)
„ 13.	Attending committee, case opened and partly proceeded with	3 3 0 to 5 5 0
	Attending Mr. —— (*a counsel*), to appoint consultation	0 10 0
	Paid his fee and clerk..	(sum paid)
	The like attendance on Mr. —— ..	0 10 0
	Paid his fee and clerk..	(sum paid)
„ 14.	Attending consultation	1 1 0
	Attending Mr. —— (*a counsel*), with minutes of evidence, and bespeaking his attendance in committee	0 10 0
	Paid his fee and clerk..	(sum paid)
	The like attendance on Mr. —— ..	0 10 0
	Paid his fee and clerk..	(sum paid)
	Attending committee, all day, witnesses examined, &c.	3 3 0 to 5 5 0
	See notes to the charges on March 18th, in respect of the Commons, as they apply as well to the Lords.	
„ 30.	Attending House of Lords on consideration of report	1 1 0
	If the solicitor is acting as parliamentary agent, he can charge 2l. 2s. for this stage.	
	If amendments on third reading:—	
	Drawing amendments, at per folio ..	0 2 0
	Forwarding same to parliamentary agent	— — —

		£	s.	d.
June 6.	Attending House when bill read third time, and passed	1	1	0
	If the solicitor is acting as parliamentary agent, he can charge 2l. 2s. for this stage.			
„ 9.	Attending House of Commons on consideration of Lords' Amendments	1	1	0
	[*No charge is allowed for attending House when bill receives the Royal Assent.*]			
„ 20.	Drawing requisition to Lord Chairman [*or* Speaker] for his certificate of bill having passed [*or*, been rejected, &c.] and copy for signature	0	10	0
	Attending therewith, and attesting his signature thereto	0	6	8
	Attending parliamentary agent therewith, and instructing him ..	0	6	8
	Sessional fee [see p. 139]	10	10	0
	But if the bill does not receive the Royal Assent, charge 2l. 2s. and upwards. *If the solicitor is also acting as parliamentary agent, he is entitled to 26l. 5s.*			
	£			

Disbursements.

[Here follow all disbursements.*]

£

* A charge, taken from the petty cash book, is generally made for incidental expenses and postages.

A Parliamentary Agent's Bill of Costs *for promoting a Private Bill.*

In Parliament,
Session 1864.

Messrs. ——, Drs.,
Solicitors,
To Messrs. ——, of ——,
Parliamentary Agents.

In all cases the charge for drawing any document includes the fair copy to keep, or for counsel to settle, no further charge is allowed for those purposes.
The charges for perusing and settling include a copy as perused and settled for own use, if required, and no copy is to be charged for the purpose of returning the same as settled.
No charge is allowed for perusal and settling by the party who charges for the drawing, but he may charge for a perusal (if necessary) of the document as settled, according to circumstances, but not in any case exceeding half the charge allowed for perusal and settling of the draft.

The following charges should be made for general attendance and time:

	£	s.	d.
Ordinary attendances	0	10	6
If upwards of an hour.. ..	1	1	0
Or, per hour	0	13	4
If required to leave London—			
Time per day	4	4	0
Hotel expenses and fares actually paid ..	1	0	0
Clerk's attendances	0	7	6

		£	s.	d.
	Attending members or peers at the House on special and necessary occasions (other than moving the stages of the bill)	1	1	0
	The charges for letters are—			
	Ordinary	0	3	6
	Containing professional advice and instructions	0	5	0
	If exceeding six folios ..	0	10	0
	See also Sessional Fee, at p. 136.			

		£	s.	d.
1863. Oct. 26.	Drawing instructions to solicitor as to contents and publication of notice	1	1	0
	Forwarding same to him	—	—	—
Nov. 4.	Perusing and settling notices for bill—			
	If less than 11 folios ..	1	1	0
	If more, according to length and other circumstances	from 1	1	0
		to 2	2	0
	Writing solicitor therewith and thereon	0	5	0
	[If parliamentary agent is acting for a local solicitor, he would make the following charges relative to publication of notice in Gazette—			
„ 10.	Having received copy notice (*generally printer's slip*) from solicitor for insertion in Gazette, attending Gazette office, directing insertion and ordering proof	0	6	8

		£	s.	d.
Nov. 10.	Examining proof	0	3	4
			to	
		0	10	0
	Returning proof and ordering publication	0	6	8
	Examining notice on publication ..	0	3	4
	And the same charges must be made if the agent has to procure the insertion in a London newspaper; except that the 3s. 4d. for examination on publication should be charged on each of the three publications.]			
„ 11.	Drawing instructions to solicitor as to form and deposit of plans ..	1	1	0
	Letter therewith to solicitor	—	—	—
„ 23.	Drawing instructions to solicitor as to form and service of notice to owners, lessees and occupiers ..	0	10	6
	Letter therewith to solicitor	—	—	—
„ 30.	Perusing and settling bill and preparing the same in parliamentary form and for press—			
	For any bill not exceeding 60 folios, according to the length of the bill and the nature and extent of revision ..		from	
		2	2	0
			to	
		5	5	0
	For any bill exceeding 60 folios and less than 150, according to the length of the bill and the nature and extent of revision		from	
		5	5	0
			to	
		10	10	0

		£ s. d.
Nov. 30.	For any bill exceeding 150 folios, according to the length of the bill and the nature and extent of revision; but if above 10*l.* 10*s.*, not exceeding (except under special circumstances) one-half the charge for drawing any such bill	5 5 0 and upwards.
	Perusing and settling clauses and amendments (according to length and other circumstances, but not exceeding 1*s. per folio*).	
	Letter therewith to solicitor	0 5 0
	Examining and making up plans and books of reference for the purpose of deposit at Parliament Office, Private Bill Office, and Board of Trade or Admiralty, each set ..	0 10 6
	Ditto—Lists of owners, &c., and other documents deposited therewith ..	0 10 6
	Attending to deposit plan, &c., at Parliament Office (Lords) and Private Bill Office (Commons), each attendance	1 1 0
	The like, at Board of Trade or Admiralty, each attendance	0 10 6
	The charge for attending to deposit includes any charge for drawing a memorandum of documents deposited, and obtaining signature of depositor thereto, and the requisite copies of the same, except the same shall exceed one folio, when 1*s.* 4*d.*	

		£ s. d.
	per folio may be charged for drawing the same, and 6d. per folio for copies to hand in to examiner, or other requisite copies; it also includes the drawing and obtaining the certificate or receipt for such deposit.	
	Attendances for the purpose of deposit cannot be charged both by parliamentary agent and solicitor.	
	The deposits described here are those generally made by the parliamentary agent; those with the clerk of the peace and parish clerks being made by the solicitor.	
Nov. 30.	Letter to solicitor that deposits had been duly made	— — —
Dec. 9.	Having received draft bill from solicitor, copy thereof for press at, per folio	0 0 6
	Attending therewith on printer with instructions as to proof	0 6 8
	When attendance to order proofs is charged, no charge is allowed for subsequent attendance to obtain proofs.	
	No attendance to be charged for ordering further additional copies.	
„ 11.	Examining print of bill—	
	Proofs	0 13 4
	or, per page of print ..	0 1 0
	Forwarding same to solicitor	— — —
„ 15.	Examining revise of bill	0 6 8
	or, per page of print	0 0 6
„ 16.	Blanking bill, drawing arrangement of sections, and finally settling bill for printer	1 1 0

		£	s.	d.
Dec. 16.	Perusing and settling petition for bill—			
	If less than 11 folios ..	1	1	0
	If more than 11 folios ..	from 1	1	0
		to 2	2	0
	Or, if the same shall exceed 50 folios, 1s. per folio upon the whole petition. A copy, as settled for own use or solicitor's, is not allowed to be charged.			
„ 18.	Letter to solicitor, as instructions relative to deposits to be made on 31st December	0	5	0
	Drawing instructions as to form of lists of owners, &c.	0	10	6
„ 21.	Perusing and settling estimate of expense [*or*, Declaration in lieu or in aid of deposit of money—Declaration and estimate—Declaration under Standing Order 41—Subscription contract] .. each	0	6	8
	Letter therewith to solicitor	—	—	—
	Having received proof of bill from solicitor, perusing alterations, and attending printer therewith ..	0	13	4
„ 22.	Drawing agent's declaration, and copies for deposit—			
	1st class bill	1	1	0
	2nd class bill	2	2	0
„ 23.	Attending at the Private Bill Office (Commons) to deposit the petition			

		£	s.	d.
	for the bill, with agent's declaration and printed copy of the bill annexed, and other printed copies of the bill, and registering the petition in the general list of petitions	1	1	0
	The making up the petition, with declaration and bill annexed, is included in the above charge.			
Dec. 23.	Letter to solicitor	—	—	—
	Attending to deposit bill at Parliament Office	1	1	0
	The like, Board of Trade [*or*, Admiralty]	0	10	6
	Attending at House with bills for Lord Chairman, his counsel and secretary	—	—	—
„ 26.	Attending printer ordering proofs of estimate [*or*, Declaration in lieu—Declaration and estimate—Declaration under Standing Order 41—Subscription contract], examining proofs and returning same with instructions to print ..	0	13	4
„ 30.	Settling requisition for warrant for deposit of money	0	6	8
	Writing solicitor therewith, and instructing him	0	5	0
„ 31.	Making up lists of owners, &c., and estimate of expense for deposit in Parliament Office	0	10	6

		£	s.	d.
Dec. 31.	The like, for deposit in Private Bill Office	0	10	6
	Attending at Parliament Office to deposit same	0	10	6
	The like, at Private Bill Office ..	0	10	6
	Attending at Vote Office to deposit printed copies of estimate ..	0	10	6
	Letter to solicitor that deposits had been duly made	—	—	—
1864. Jan. 9.	Attending at Private Bill Office to ascertain if any memorial against this bill on Standing Orders, and found there was one	—	—	—
	Attending, ordering copy thereof ..	0	7	6
„ 11.	Settling warrant for payment of parliamentary deposit, and attending at Private Bill Office to get same executed	0	10	0
	Drawing affidavit, verifying signature to warrant	0	6	8
	Clerk attending to be sworn	0	7	6
	Attending at accountant-general's to deposit same and bespeak directions	0	10	6
„ 12.	Attending for and obtaining his directions for payment into Court, and subsequently attending broker and making arrangement for transfer .	1	1	0

Date		£	s.	d.
Jan. 14.	Attending in City and at Bank of England with parties making transfer (engaged upwards of an hour)	1	1	0
„ 16.	Attending, bespeaking certificate of amount paid into Court, and afterwards for same	0	10	6
	The last four charges can only be made by the person who actually acted; if the solicitor did, then the agent must not charge, and vice versâ.			
	Settling form of affidavit as to deposit with clerk of the peace	0	6	8
	The like, with parish clerks	0	6	8
	The like, as to applications to owners.	0	6	8
	No charge is allowed for copies.			
	Forwarding same to solicitor	—	—	—
„ 17.	Perusing [*or* drawing] statement of proofs, and forwarding same to solicitor, and instructing him—			
	1st class bill	1	1	0
	Ditto—where lands and houses are taken ..	1	11	6
	2nd class bill	2	2	0
„ 21.	Having received statement of proofs from solicitor, together with documents referred to therein, perusing and finally arranging same for proof before examiner—			
	1st class bill	0	10	6
	2nd class bill	1	1	0

		£	s.	d.
Jan. 21.	One copy thereof for own use before examiner—			
	Two copies thereof for examiner, at per folio	0	0	6
„ 28.	Attending before examiner, case in the list, but not called on	2	2	0
„ 29.	Attending before examiner to prove compliance with Standing Orders —Memorial of —— inquired into, and examiner decided that the Standing Orders had not been complied with	from 3 to 5	3 to 5	0 to 0
	[If the petition is unopposed this charge will be—			
	In 1st class bills	2	2	0
	In 2nd class bills	3	3	0
	or, If a petition is adjourned for further proofs, each subsequent attendance, when the examiner shall inquire into the same, or attending to apply for a postponement or adjournment ..	1	1	0]

When two or more petitions for bills, being promoted or opposed by or on behalf of the same clients, are appointed for consideration by the same examiner on the same day, but are not called on, the agents of such clients will not be entitled to such charge in respect of each petition for a bill so promoted or opposed, but may charge any sum not exceeding 1l. 1s. for additional trouble (if any) in respect of each other petition for a bill on the same list; provided that in no case (except under special circumstances) shall a charge exceeding 5l. 5s. be made in respect of one such day's attendance on behalf of the same clients.

		£	s.	d.
Jan. 29.	Attendance of clerk to give evidence .	0	10	6
	[If in favour of or against an opposed bill, or in support of or against allegations of a memorial	1	1	0]
	Only one attendance is allowed to be charged for proofs before the examiner in respect of the Standing Orders of both Houses, when the same are taken simultaneously.			
Feb. 4.	Attending, ordering copy of examiner's report	0	7	6
„ 5.	Attending meeting of Lord Chairman and Chairman of Ways and Means relative to the Houses in which the bills should commence, when it was ordered that this should commence in the Commons	1	1	0
	Attending to obtain petition for bill from the Private Bill Office, and get the same presented and petition referred to Standing Orders Committee [*or*, bill ordered, or other proceeding thereon] ..	1	1	0
	The attendance at the House on the member who presents the petition is included in this charge.			
„ 8.	Forwarding copy of examiner's report to solicitor	—	—	—
„ 11.	Having received draft statement for Standing Orders Committee (Commons) from solicitor, perusing and settling same	from 0	6	8
		to 1	1	0
	or, per sheet of 10 folios ..	0	6	8

		£	s.	d.
Feb. 11.	Three copies thereof for use of committee .. at per folio..	0	0	6
„ 12.	Attending Standing Orders Committee, when they resolved on reporting in favour of dispensing with Standing Orders	2	2	0
	Attending printer, instructing him to print bill with names of members thereon	0	6	8
	Making up bill in parliamentary form for House, and deposit of the same	1	1	0
	Attending to deposit prints of bill in Private Bill Office	—	—	—
	The like, with doorkeepers	—	—	—
„ 15.	Attending House of Commons when bill read first time	1	1	0
	This includes drawing motion for leave and attending member at House who makes the motion.			
	Notice of second reading for Monday .	—	—	—
„ 22.	Attending House when bill read second time and referred to Committee of Selection [*or*, General Committee on Railway and Canal Bills] ..	1	1	0
	This includes attending the member at the House who makes the motion.			
	Perusing and considering Lord Chairman's remarks on bill	0 to 1	10 to 1	6 to 0
	Copy thereof for solicitor	0	6	8
	or, per folio..	0	0	4

		£	s.	d.
Feb. 22.	The like, for use	0	6	8
	or, per folio ..	0	0	4
„ 23.	Attending solicitor, conferring and advising on Lord Chairman's remarks on bill, upwards of one hour	1	1	0
	Attending to order and obtain copy of a petition [*or* petitions] against bill	0	7	6
	Only one attendance is allowed to be charged for ordering and obtaining any number of petitions against the same bill at the same time.			
	Perusing same—			
	If under twenty folios	0	6	8
	If above, per folio ..	0	0	4
	Making copy thereof, for use, at per folio	0	0	6
	The like for solicitor, at per folio ..	0	0	6
	Letter therewith to solicitor	—	—	—
„ 24.	Attending Chairman of Ways and Means [*or* Speaker] with reference to certain clauses	1	1	0
„ 25.	Perusing and settling bill for deposit, according to Lord Chairman's requirements	1	1	0
	Perusing and settling draft statement for Standing Orders Committee (Lords) in favour of dispensing with Standing Orders	0 to 1	6 to 1	8 to 0
	or, per sheet of ten folios ..	0	6	8

		£ s. d.
Feb. 26.	Attending Standing Orders Committee (Lords) when they resolved on reporting in favour of dispensing with the Standing Orders ..	2 2 0
	Attending to lay copy of bill before Committee of Selection	— — —
„ 27.	Attending Committee of Selection [*or* Committee on Railway and Canal Bills] on nomination of committee and arrangement of groups ..	1 1 0
	If the committee adjourn without reading the bill, same charge may be made.	
	Attending, obtaining and subsequently perusing report of Board of Trade on bill	0 10 6
„ 28.	Attending Mr. Speaker's counsel to go through bill	1 1 0
	This is for the first attendance; if subsequent attendances are necessary, 10s. 6d. must be charged.	
Mar. 1.	Attending Lord Chairman and his counsel, going through bill ..	1 1 0
	or, per hour ..	0 13 4
„ 2.	Perusing and settling petition in favour of bill and returning same to solicitor	0 6 8
	And so on for each petition.	

If a petition for additional provision is necessary the following are the charges :—

		£ s. d.
Mar. 3.	Perusing and settling petition for additional provision—	
	If less than 11 folios ..	1 1 0
	If more than 11 folios ..	from 1 1 0 to 2 2 0
	Or, if the same shall exceed 50 folios, 1s. per folio upon the whole petition. The like clauses annexed, according to length, &c., but not exceeding 1s. per folio.	
	Attending printer, instructing him and ordering proofs of clauses ..	0 13 4
	Letter to solicitor therewith	— — —
	If notices are published and plans, &c. are deposited, the charges are the same as for complying with the Standing Orders in those particulars previously to introduction of bill.	
„ 4.	Attending House, petition presented and referred to examiner ..	1 1 0
	Attending examiner for appointment	— — —
	Perusing [*or* drawing] statement of proofs, and finally arranging same	from 1 1 0 to 2 2 0
„ 7.	Attending examiner, same inquired into—	
	If unopposed	1 1 0
	If opposed	2 2 0 to 3 3 0
	If opposed, and also if necessary to go before the Standing Orders Committee, the charges, with the exception of the above attendance, are the same as on the petition for the bill.	

		£	s.	d.
Mar. 7.	Attending at the Private Bill Office to deposit petitions in favour of bill, and registering the same, viz.,			
	If one petition, or less than three	0	10	6
	If three petitions, and less than seven	1	1	0
	If seven petitions, and less than twelve	1	11	6
	For any number exceeding twelve	2	2	0
	The endorsing petitions and preparing the same for deposit are included in the above fees.			
„ 8.	Filling up copies of bills with alterations as proposed to be submitted to committee, for Lord Chairman, —his Counsel,—Chairman of Ways and Means,—Counsel to Speaker,—Solicitor,—and Private Bill Office:			
	For the first copy, unless the amendments be very numerous	0	6	8
	For each other copy, unless the amendments be very numerous	0	3	4
	If new clauses or amendments be added, exceeding six folios, copies of the same may be charged at 6d. per folio.			

		£	s.	d.
Mar. 15.	The like for use in committee and parties	—	—	—
	Five copies are allowed for the committee, and one for the clerk, in opposed cases.			
	Drawing report from committee on bill	0	10	6
	Two fair copies	0	5	0
„ 16.	Attending consultation with counsel (if required)	1	1	0
	Attending committee on group, but this bill not reached	2	2	0
„ 17.	Attending consultation with counsel (if required)	1	1	0
	Attending committee when preamble of bill considered	2	2	0
	But when the clauses are considered	from 3	3	0
		to 5	5	0
	[The following are the other charges an agent would make:—			
	In an unopposed bill ..	from 2	2	0
		to 3	3	0
	To apply for a postponement, &c.	1	1	0
	In an opposed bill, without counsel	from 3	3	0
		to 5	5	0]

[If the clauses on petition for additional provision are allowed, there will be copies thereof for the committee, same as of bill, and

		£	s.	d.
	attending committee on bill when they are added.]			
	[Filling up bills with amendments as resettled, for use of the committee, before its final meeting are sometimes charged; and after the committee is over amendments as finally agreed to are charged as follows,—one for report,—one for Chairman of Ways and Means,—one for Speaker's counsel,—one for press,—one for Lord Chairman,—one for his counsel, and, in certain cases, one for Board of Trade.]			
Apr. 20.	Attending committee clerk with bill for report	—	—	—
„ 21.	Attending House when bill reported ..	1	1	0
	Attending to lay amended bills before the Chairman of Ways and Means and Speaker's counsel	—	—	—
	Attending printer, instructing him to print bill	0	6	8
	No charge is allowed for subsequent attendance to obtain proofs. *No attendance to be charged for ordering further additional copies.*			
„ 23.	Two clerks attending at Private Bill Office examining and correcting proof print of bill with committee bill—			
	at per page of print ..	—	—	—
	1s. for each clerk ..	0	2	0

		£	s.	d.
Apr. 23.	Settling arrangement of clauses, and copy for press	1	1	0
	Attending printer, instructing him to print revises	0	6	8
	Examining same	0	6	8
	or, per page	0	0	6
	Attending printer with instructions to print off copies	0	6	8
„ 24.	Attending Private Bill Office with House copies of bill for clerk's examination	—	—	—
	Subsequently attending to ascertain if correct	—	—	—
	Notice consideration amended bill for —— next..	—	—	—
„ 25.	Attending House on consideration of report	1	1	0
„ 27.	Attending House of Commons on bill being read third time and passed.	1	1	0
	Attending House of Lords on bill being read first time and referred to the examiners..	1	1	0
„ 28.	Marking on print of bill the amendments made therein for examiner . *A manuscript copy of the amendments is not allowed to be charged.*	0	6	8
	Attending examiner for appointment .	—	—	—

		£	s.	d.
Apr. 29.	Attending to order and obtain copies of petition of —— against this bill in the Lords	0	7	6
	Only one attendance is allowed to be charged for ordering and obtaining any number of petitions against the same bill at the same time.			
May 3.	Perusing and settling statement of proofs before examiner, of compliance with Standing Orders, not previously inquired into ..	from 1	1	0
		to 2	2	0
	The charges relative to affidavits, copies, memorial, &c., if required, are the same as on introduction of bill.			
„ 4.	Attending examiner, further proofs given and Standing Orders found complied with—			
	If unopposed	1	1	0
	If opposed	2	2	0
		to 3	3	0
	If the Standing Orders are found not to have been complied with, the charges incidental to the Standing Orders Committee will be the same as on the introduction of the bill, which see.			
	Clerk attending to give evidence ..	0	10	6
„ 7.	Attending House of Lords, bill read second time, and committed ..	1	1	0
„ 8.	Attending House till its rising to ascertain if committee appointed ..	0	7	6
	And the like charge for each day this is done.			

		£	s.	d.
May 8.	Committee on bill— *[The attendance charges incidental to the committee are the same as in the Commons, which see on March 16th.]*			
„ 26.	Attending to get bill reported ..	1	1	0
	Attending printer with bill as passed Lords' Committee, instructing him	0	6	8
„ 27.	Filling up bills with amendments as passed committee, viz.: one for Lord Chairman,—one for his counsel,—one for Chairman of Ways and Means,—one for Speaker's counsel,—one for Private Bill Office,—one for Journal Office—			
	For the first copy, unless the amendments be very numerous	0	6	8
	For each other copy, unless the amendments be very numerous	0	3	4
	If new clauses or amendments be added, exceeding six folios, copies of the same may be charged at 6d. per folio.			
	Attending them therewith	—	—	—
„ 30.	If amendments on third reading, perusing and settling amendments to be proposed on third reading— *(According to length and other circumstances, but not exceeding 1s. per folio.)*			

		£	s.	d.
May 30.	Attending printer therewith, instructing him, and examining proofs and returning same	0	13	4
June 6.	Attending House of Lords, bill read third time and passed	1	1	0
	Drawing paper of amendments made in Lords, in extenso, for printer of votes	1	1	0
	Copy thereof	0	13	4
„ 7.	Attending Chairman of Ways and Means when he sanctioned Lords' amendments	1	1	0
	The like, Speaker's counsel	0	10	6
„ 9.	Attending House of Commons when Lords' amendments agreed to ..	1	1	0
„ 10.	Attending to get bill returned to Lords agreed to	1	1	0
„ 15.	Preparing bill for press as it received royal assent, and attending printer therewith, instructing him ..	0	10	6
„ 20.	Having received from solicitor requisition for Lord Chairman [*or* Speaker's] certificate, drawing same and copy for signature, and attending House to procure signature	0	10	0
	Drawing and copy affidavit verifying signature	0	10	0

		£	s.	d.
June 30.	Clerk attending to be sworn	0	7	6
	Forwarding same to solicitor ..	—	—	—
	Sessional fee [see p. 136, for attendances, &c. included in it] .. *But if the bill does not receive the royal assent, charge 2l. 2s. and upwards.*	26	5	0

Disbursements.

[Here follow all disbursements.*]

£

£

* A charge, taken from the petty cash book, is generally made for postages and incidental expenses.

An Attorney's or Solicitor's Bill of Costs *for opposing a Private Bill.*

In Parliament,
Session 1864.

The —— Company, Drs.,

To —— ,

Solicitors,

of ——.

In respect of the opposition in Parliament, on behalf of the said Company to the —— Act:—

[*Attendance and general charges as at p. 21.*]

1863.		£	s.	d.
Nov. 26.	Notice having been published of the intention of the —— company to apply to parliament for a bill, attending secretary conferring on effect that the proposed line would have on the company's property, upwards of an hour ..	1	1	0
„ 28.	Attending board in conference on notice of proposed bill, when we were instructed to communicate with the solicitor for the bill ..	1	1	0
„ 29.	Letter to solicitor for bill asking interview on bill	0	3	6

		£	s.	d.
Dec. 3.	Attending Mr. ——, the solicitor for the bill, when he declined to furnish any further information as to its details than we already had in the notice	0	13	4
„ 10.	Attending board conferring on course to be taken, when it was resolved to wait deposit of bill, and in meantime to communicate with parliamentary agent	1	1	0
	Attending meeting of directors and advising as to the opposition ..	0	13	4
	Letter to parliamentary agent upon proposed opposition	0	5	0
„ 27.	Perusing print of bill forwarded by parliamentary agent, and comparing, engaged two hours ..	1	6	8
	Same with notice and making notes.			
„ 28.	Journey to —— with Mr. ——, engineer, examining plans and books of reference deposited with clerk of the peace, when we discovered many important non-compliances.	2	2	0
	Fares, &c. ..	(as paid)		
	[If a local solicitor—			
„ 30.	Journey to London to consult parliamentary agent, and discussing subject of opposition with him—			
	Time, per day	4	4	0
	Hotel expenses, per day .	1	1	0
	Fares, &c.	(sum paid)]		

		£ s. d.
Dec. 30.	It having been determined to oppose on Standing Orders, two clerks employed —— days checking reference on the ground and obtaining information—	
	Time per day, each clerk ..	1 11 6
	Hotel and other expenses ..	(sum paid)
1864.		
Jan. 4.	Letter with memorial to parliamentary agent to settle	0 3 6
	Attending you conferring	0 13 4
„ 8.	Having received memorial from parliamentary agent as settled, engrossing same, at per folio ..	0 0 9
	Attending secretary, getting seal of company affixed to memorial ..	0 13 4
	Or, if necessary, to procure different signatures to the memorial, a clerk should be preferred to a principal.	
	Letter to agent therewith	0 3 6
	[Or if solicitor is acting as parliamentary agent—	
	Attending at the Private Bill Office to deposit memorials, and registering the same, viz.:—	
	If one memorial, or less than three	0 13 4
	If three, and less than seven..	1 1 0

		£	s.	d.
	If seven, and less than twelve	1	11	6
	For any number exceeding twelve	2	2	0
	The endorsing memorials and preparing the same for deposit are included in the above fees, except when the same are prepared by the solicitor, when from 3s. 4d. to 6s. 8d. is allowed for endorsing a memorial, or set, and transmitting the same to the parliamentary agent for the purpose of deposit.]			
Jan. 15.	Long letter to parliamentary agent as to evidence to be adduced in support of memorial	0	10	0
" 20.	Parliamentary agent having forwarded a copy of memorial with their observations thereon, going through same and making additional notes thereon, engaged upwards of an hour	1	1	0
" 25.	Attending before the examiner when the petition for the bill was in the list, but was not called on ..	2	2	0
	When two or more petitions for bills, being promoted or opposed by or on behalf of the same clients, are appointed for consideration by the same examiner on the same day, but are not called on, the solicitors of such clients will not be entitled to such charge in respect of each petition for a bill so promoted or opposed, but may charge any sum not exceeding 1l. 1s. for additional trouble (if any) in respect of each other petition for a bill on the same list; provided that in no case (except under special circumstances) shall a charge			

		£ s. d.
	exceeding 5l. 5s. be made in respect of one such day's attendance on behalf of the same clients.	
Jan. 26.	Attending before the examiner when an appearance was entered on this memorial, but same was not called on	2 2 0 to 3 3 0
	When a solicitor appears and attends for two or more memorials, complaining of non-compliance with the Standing Orders, on behalf of the same clients, against the same bill, he will be entitled to charge one day's attendance only in respect of the same.	
„ 27.	Attending before the examiner when memorial inquired into	from 3 3 0 to 5 5 0
	[Or if a local solicitor—	
	Journey to town when arranging as to course to be pursued before the examiner, and when case inquired into by examiner, who decided that the Standing Orders had not been complied with—	
	Time, per day	4 4 0
	Hotel expenses	1 1 0
	Fares, &c.	(sum paid)]
Feb. 4.	Long attendance at board conferring on result as to Standing Orders inquiry	1 1 0
„ 6.	Having received copy of examiner's report, perusing same	0 10 6

		£ s. d.
Feb. 8.	Drawing statement for Standing Orders Committee (according to length, &c.)	from 0 13 4 to 2 2 0
	[If solicitor is acting as parliamentary agent, he may charge the following—	
	Three copies of statement for committee, and use, at per folio ..	0 0 6
„ 9.	Attending engineer, conferring on general nature of injury to the company's property that would be done by the proposed line, when it was arranged that he should prepare a report on the subject for the directors (upwards of an hour)	1 1 0
„ 11.	Attending engineer, conferring upon points in report and arranging marginal observations thereon, engaged three hours, at 13*s.* 4*d.* per hour	2 0 0
	Attending Mr. —— (*a counsel*), appointing consultation	0 10 0
	Paid his fee and clerk..	(sum paid)
„ 12.	Letter to parliamentary agent requesting him to attend consultation with counsel	0 3 6
„ 13.	Attending consultation on general course of opposition to this bill..	1 1 0

		£	s.	d.
Feb. 19.	Instructions for petition against, and praying to be heard by counsel..	0	13	4
	Drawing petition—			
	If less than eleven folios..	1	1	0
	If more, per folio.. ..	0	2	0
	Letter to agent therewith and thereon	0	5	0
	[If a London solicitor—			
„ 20.	Attending Standing Orders Committee, when committee decided to report in favour of the Standing Orders being dispensed with	2	2	0]
	[*Or*, if local solicitor—			
	Perusing letter from parliamentary agent, stating that the Standing Orders Committee of the Commons had dispensed with the Standing Orders in this case ..	—	—	—]
	Attending chairman, conferring and advising	0	13	4
	Drawing petition against, by persons locally interested, but not praying to be heard by counsel—			
	If less than eleven folios ..	0	13	4
	If less than fifteen folios ..	1	0	0
	If more than fifteen folios, per sheet	0	13	4
	or per folio ..	0	1	4
„ 22.	Having received petitions as settled, ingrossing same for lodging in the House of Commons, at per folio	0	0	9

		£	s.	d.
Feb. 22.	Copy thereof for agent, at per folio ..	0	0	6
	Copy thereof for each counsel, not exceeding three counsel, at per folio	0	0	6
„ 23.	Attending various persons, procuring their signatures to petitions— Three hours at 13*s.* 4*d.* per hour	2	0	0
	From 3s. 4d. to 6s. 8d. is allowed for endorsing a petition or set of petitions, and transmitting the same to the parliamentary agent for the purpose of deposit (except when included in the sessional fee).			
	[If the solicitor is acting as parliamentary agent, he will charge the following—			
	Attending at the Private Bill Office to deposit petitions against bill, and registering the same, viz.:—			
	If one petition, or less than three	0	13	4
	If three petitions, and less than seven	1	1	0
	If seven petitions, and less than twelve	1	11	6
	For any number exceeding twelve	2	2	0
	The endorsing petitions and preparing the same for deposit are included in the above fees, except when the same are prepared by the solicitor.			

		£ s. d.
Feb. 29.	Three copies, statement for Lords' Standing Orders Committee, at per folio	0 0 6
	Drawing already charged for in Commons.]	
Mar. 4.	Attending Standing Orders Committee when committee decided on reporting in favour of Standing Orders being dispensed with ..	2 2 0
	[*Or*, if local solicitor—	
	Perusing letter from parliamentary agent that Lords' Standing Orders Committee had dispensed with the Standing Orders	— — —]
	The charges for the brief, proofs of witnesses, attending counsel to pay fees and so forth, are the same as will be found at p. 40.	
„ 7.	Attending consultation with counsel..	1 1 0
	Attending to watch proceedings of committee, but bill not reached ..	1 1 0
	In no case (except under special circumstances) must a charge exceeding 5l. 5s. be made in respect of attending to watch proceedings in the case of petitions against a bill, previously to such petitions being considered.	
„ 8.	Attending consultation with counsel..	1 1 0
	Attending committee, preamble of bill considered	from 3 3 0 to 5 5 0

		£ s. d.
Mar. 9.	Attending consultation with counsel..	1 1 0
	Attending committee when bill passed committee..	from 3 3 0 to 5 5 0

When a solicitor appears and attends for two or more petitions against a bill, on behalf of the same clients, he will be entitled to charge one day's attendance only in respect of the same.

When two or more bills, being promoted or opposed by or on behalf of the same clients, are appointed for consideration by the committee on the same day, but are postponed or adjourned without being considered, or are not separately considered by the committee, the solicitors of such clients respectively will not be entitled to such charge in respect of each bill, so promoted or opposed; but may charge any sum not exceeding 1l. 1s. for additional trouble (if any) in respect of each other bill so postponed or adjourned, or not separately considered; provided that in no case (except under special circumstances) shall a charge exceeding 5l. 5s. be made in respect of one such day's attendance upon the committee on behalf of the same clients.

No charge is allowed for attendance of a clerk to the solicitor on a committee, except for the purpose of being examined as a witness.

[*Or*, if local solicitor—

„ 28.	Journey to London, conferring on bill and attending committee on bill, when the bill passed through the committee—	
	Time, per day ..	4 4 0
	Hotel expenses ..	1 1 0
	Fares, &c. ..	..(sum paid)]

		£	s.	d.
April 4.	Having received prints of bill as reported by the committee, perusing same, upwards of an hour ..	1	1	0
„ 6.	Attending board, conferring on result of opposition in Commons when it was determined to pursue the opposition in the Lords, engaged two hours..	1	6	8
	Letter to agent hereon, and instructing him accordingly	0	5	0
„ 7.	Instructions for petition against bill in House of Lords, and praying to be heard by counsel	0	13	4
	Drawing petition—			
	If less than eleven folios..	1	1	0
	If more than eleven folios, per folio	0	2	0
	Letter therewith, to agent to settle ..	0	3	6
„ 9.	Attending board, reading over petition against, in Lords, and conferring generally on opposition, upwards of an hour	1	1	0
„ 10.	Letter to Mr. ——, as to his willingness to attend House of Lords to repeat his evidence given in other House	0	5	0
„ 11.	Parliamentary agent having returned petition against, settled, engrossing same for presentation in House of Lords, at per folio ..	0	0	9

		£	s.	d.
April 11.	Copy thereof for agent, at per folio ..	0	0	6
	Copies for each counsel, not exceeding three, at per folio	0	0	6
„ 12.	Various attendances, procuring signatures to petition, engaged two hours	1	6	8
„ 15.	Instructions for brief	—	—	—
	For the charges relative to the brief, proofs, &c., see p. 40.			
„ 20.	Attending secretary, communicating arrangements as to opposing bill in Lords, and day it was likely the committee of that House would meet	0	13	4
„ 25.	Long interview with engineer as to various matters in connection with opposition..	0	13	4
„ 28.	Letter from agent naming day appointed for meeting of committee	—	—	—
May 9.	Attending consultation with counsel..	1	1	0
	Attending committee (Lords), when committee ultimately adjourned to enable us to agree with the promoters as to clauses to be inserted in our favour	from 3 to 5	3 to 5	0 to 0
„ 10.	Instructions for clauses	0	13	4
	Drawing clauses, per folio	0	2	0

		£	s.	d.
May 10.	Conferring with parliamentary agent thereon, and subsequently with solicitor and agent of promoters, when same agreed to, two hours	1	6	8
„ 12.	Attending consultation with counsel..	1	1	0
	Attending committee, when clauses inserted and bill passed	3 to 5	3 to 5	0 0
	[If a local solicitor, journey to London, &c., instead of foregoing, as at p. 80.]			
„ 17.	Long attendance on Mr. ——, the solicitor for the bill in conference, on effect of clauses inserted in bill on behalf of our company ..	0	13	4
„ 21.	Letter to parliamentary agent for information hereon	0	5	0
	No sessional fee is allowed, in the case of oppositions (see p. 139), but a small charge is usually made "for attendances, letters, &c., not otherwise charged."			
	£			

Disbursements.

£

£

A PARLIAMENTARY AGENT'S BILL OF COSTS *for opposing a Private Bill.*

In Parliament,
SESSION 1864.

MESSRS. ——,

SOLICITORS, DRS.,

TO MESSRS. ——,

Parliamentary Agents.

In respect of the opposition in Parliament, on behalf of —— to the —— Act:—

[*Attendances and general charges as at p. 48.*]

		£	s.	d.
1863.				
Dec. 30.	Attending solicitor, going through notice for bill, examining plans, &c., and advising on opposition, upwards of an hour	1	1	0
1864.				
Jan. 5.	Perusing and settling memorial forwarded by solicitor—			
	If less than eleven folios..	1	1	0
	If more than eleven folios	from 1	1	0
		to 2	2	0
	(Or if the same shall exceed fifty folios, 1*s.* per folio upon the whole memorial.)			
" 5.	Letter therewith to solicitor	0	5	0

		£	s.	d.
Jan. 9.	Having received memorial from solicitor—			
	Attending at the Private Bill Office to deposit memorial, and registering the same, viz.:—			
	If one memorial, or less than three	0	10	6
	If three, and less than seven	1	1	0
	If seven, and less than twelve	1	11	6
	For any number exceeding twelve	2	2	0
	The endorsing petitions and preparing the same for deposit are included in the above fees.			
„ 20.	Attending solicitor and engineer, conferring on course of proceeding before examiner, upwards of an hour	1	1	0
	Attending Private Bill Office, taking out appearance on this memorial	0	7	6
	Only one charge to be made for taking out appearances on any number of petitions from the same clients on the same day.			
„ 25.	Attending examiner, petition in list, but not called on	2	2	0
	When two or more petitions for bills, being promoted or opposed by or on behalf of the same clients, are appointed for consideration by the same examiner on the same day, but are not called on, the agents of such clients respectively will not be entitled to such charge in respect of			

		£ s. d.
	each petition for a bill so promoted or opposed, but may charge any sum not exceeding 1l. 1s. for additional trouble (if any) in respect of each other petition for a bill on the same list; provided that in no case (except under special circumstances) shall a charge exceeding 5l. 5s. be made in respect of one such day's attendance on behalf of the same clients.	
Jan. 26.	Attending examiner, entering appearance upon memorial, but same not called on	from 2 2 0 to 3 3 0
	When an agent appears and attends for two or more memorials, complaining of non-compliance with the Standing Orders, on behalf of the same clients, against the same bill, he will be entitled to charge one day's attendance only, in respect of the same.	
„ 27.	Attending examiner, memorial inquired into and the examiner decided that the Standing Orders had not been complied with	from 3 3 0 to 5 5 0
Feb. 3.	Attending, ordering copy of examiner's report, and subsequently for same	0 7 6
„ 5.	Perusing examiner's report	0 10 6
	Long letter to solicitor, advising as to statement for Standing Orders Committee	0 10 0
„ 9.	Perusing and settling statement for Standing Orders Committee, against dispensing with Standing Orders	from 0 6 8 to 1 1 0

		£	s.	d.
Feb. 9.	Making three fair copies of statement for committee and use, at per folio	0	0	6
	Attending clerk to Standing Orders Committee (Commons) with statement	0	7	6
„ 13.	Attending consultation with counsel upon general course of this opposition	1	1	0
„ 20.	Attending Standing Orders Committee, when committee decided to report in favour of dispensing with the Standing Orders ..	2	2	0
	Letter to solicitor that this bill was read a 1st time, and as to the last day for depositing petitions against it	0	5	0
	Perusing and settling petition against bill—			
	If less than eleven folios..	1	1	0
	If more than eleven folios	from 1	1	0
		to 2	2	0
	(Or if the same shall exceed fifty folios, 1s. per folio upon the whole petition.)			
„ 25.	Having received petitions against from solicitor, attending, depositing same in Private Bill Office, and registering same—			
	If one petition, or less than three..	0	10	6

		£	s.	d.
	If three petitions, or less than seven	1	1	0
	If seven petitions, and less than twelve	1	11	6
	For any number exceeding twelve	2	2	0
	The endorsing petitions and preparing the same for deposit are included in the above fees.			
Feb. 29.	Making three copies, statement for Lords Standing Order Committee and use, at per folio	0	0	6
	Attending Parliament Office, depositing statement	0	7	6
Mar. 4.	Attending Standing Orders Committee (Lords) when committee decided on reporting in favour of Standing Orders being dispensed with	2	2	0
	Attending Committee of Selection (or, General Committee on Railway and Canal Bills) watching proceedings, when this bill was grouped	1	1	0
	Attending to obtain report of said committee, showing proposed grouping, perusing same and forwarding same to solicitor ..	0	10	6
	Attending to obtain Board of Trade report on bill, and perusing same	0	10	6

		£	s.	d.
Mar. 4.	Attending Committee of Selection (or, General Committee on Railways and Canals) when they fixed the meeting of the committee ..	1	1	0
„ 7.	Attending consultation with counsel..	1	1	0
	Attending at Private Bill Office, taking out appearance upon this petition	0	7	6
	Attending to watch proceedings of committee, but bill not reached..	1	1	0
	In no case (except under special circumstances) must a charge exceeding 5l. 5s. be made in respect of attending to watch proceedings in the case of petitions against a bill, previously to such petitions being considered.			
	Attending consultation with counsel..	1	1	0
	Attending committee, entering appearance on petition, and preamble of bill was considered ..	2	2	0
„ 8.	Attending consultation with counsel..	1	1	0
„ 9.	Attending committee when bill passed the committee	from 3 to 5	3 5	0 0

When an agent appears and attends for two or more petitions against a bill, on behalf of the same clients, he will be entitled to charge one day's attendance only, in respect of the same.

When two or more bills, being promoted or opposed by or on behalf of the same clients, are appointed for consideration by the committee on the same day, but are postponed or adjourned without being considered, or are not separately considered by the committee, the agents of such clients respectively will not be entitled to

		£	s.	d.
	such charge in respect of each bill, so promoted or opposed; but may charge any sum not exceeding 1l. 1s. for additional trouble (if any) in respect of each other bill so postponed or adjourned, or not separately considered; provided that in no case (except under special circumstances) shall a charge exceeding 5l. 5s. be made in respect of one such day's attendance upon the committee on behalf of the same clients.			
April 3.	Attending to bespeak, and afterwards to obtain filled up bill as passed committee..	0	7	6
„ 10.	Perusing and settling petition against, in the Lords—			
	If less than eleven folios..	1	1	0
	If more than eleven folios	from 1	1	0
		to 2	2	0
	(Or, if the same shall exceed fifty folios, 1s. per folio upon the whole petition.)			
	Forwarding same to solicitor, with letter thereon	0	5	0
„ 19.	Attending House of Lords, when committee appointed to meet on the ——	0	10	6
	Attending solicitor, informing thereof	0	7	6
May 9.	Attending committee office, taking out appearance on this petition ..	0	7	6
	Attending consultation with counsel..	1	1	0

		£ s. d.
May 9.	Attending committee (Lords) when committee ultimately adjourned to enable us to agree with promoters as to certain clauses ..	from 3 3 0 to 5 5 0
„ 10.	Attending solicitor on clauses, and finally settling same, two hours..	1 6 8
„ 12.	Attending consultation with counsel..	1 1 0
	Attending committee, clauses inserted and bill passed	3 3 0 to 5 5 0
	No sessional fee is allowed in oppositions, but a small charge is usually allowed for attendances at Houses, watching proceedings, and to pay fees, messages, &c.	from 1 1 0 to 5 5 0
	£	

Disbursements.

£

£

A Local Attorney or Solicitor's Bill of Costs *for Promoting a Private Bill of the First Class under the Standing Orders.*

The black marginal line means charges incident to opposed cases.

In Parliament,
Session 1864.

The —— Company, Drs.,

To Messrs. ——, of ——,

Solicitors.

In respect of the Promotion, in Parliament, on behalf of the said Company, of the —— Act, 1864.

1863.		£	s.	d.
Oct. 12.	Attending you, receiving instructions to communicate with parliamentary agents as to bill, and conferring with you thereon	0	13	4
	Long and special letter to agent stating objects of proposed bill	0	10	0
„ 14.	Having received reply from him—			
	Instructions for notice for Gazette ..	0	13	4
	Drawing notice—			
	If less than eleven folios	1	1	0
	If more, per folio ..	0	2	0

		£	s.	d.
Oct. 14.	Long and special letter to parliamentary agent therewith	0	5	0
„ 19.	Attending you with notice as returned settled, and conferring thereon ..	0	13	4
	Copy notice for insertion in each newspaper, at per folio	0	0	6
	Attending each newspaper office, [or forwarding same if at distance,] with instructions	0	6	8
	If a journey to a town where a newspaper is published becomes necessary, the charge is, for a clerk, from 1l. 1s. to 2l. 2s. day time, and expenses and fares out of pocket; but such journies are not justifiable if a letter would answer the purpose.			
„ 23.	Examining proofs when returned, each proof	0 to 0	3 to 10	4 to 0
	Returning proof, and ordering insertion for three weeks, or otherwise ..	0	6	8
	If a revise is necessary, an addition for ordering revise and examining same, of each revise	0	10	0
	No other or further charge is allowed with reference to printing the notice.			
	Letter to parliamentary agent with notice for insertion in Gazette	—	—	—
	All ordinary communications of this nature with the agent are covered by the sessional fee.			
„ 27.	Examining notice on its first insertion in newspaper	0	3	4
„ 29.	Long attendance on you with reference to bill..	0	13	4

		£	s.	d.
Nov. 3.	Examining notice, on its second insertion in newspaper	0	3	4
„ 7.	Attending Mr. ——, who called for some information as to bill	0	13	4
„ 10.	Examining notice, on its insertion in newspaper	0	3	4
Dec. 2.	Instructions for bill	2	2	0
	Drawing same, at per folio	0	2	0
	And additional clauses at same rate. As the bill is printed in London the charges incidental to that process are made by the agent.			
	Letter to agent therewith	—	—	—
„ 9.	Having received print of bill from agent, conferring with you thereon ..	0	13	4
„ 16.	Drawing petition for bill—			
	If less than eleven folios ..	1	1	0
	If more, per folio	0	2	0
	Writing agent therewith to settle ..	0	5	0
	Ingrossing petition on its return from agent, at per folio	0	0	9
	Attending Mr. ——, obtaining his signature to petition..	0	13	4
	Attending Mr. ——, who called to sign same	0	6	8
	Forwarding same to agent	—	—	—
	Attending you in long conference on draft bill	0	13	4

		£	s.	d.
Dec. 17.	Journey to London to confer with parliamentary agent on bill, and future proceedings thereon—			
	Time, at per day	4	4	0
	Hotel expenses, at per day	1	1	0
	Fares, &c.	(sum paid)		
	Travelling at night is generally reckoned as a day. *This charge covers all work done in the time, and no detailed charges during the period must be made, excepting if done at home by a partner or clerk; a time charge is not allowed for Sundays, but hotel expenses only.*			
„ 22.	Having received telegram from parliamentary agent relative to clause 12, drawing telegram in answer, and attending telegraph office despatching same	0	10	0
	Long attendance conferring with you on clauses 12 and 13	0	13	4
	Letter to parliamentary agent thereon	0	5	0
1864.				
Jan. 6.	Drawing [*or* if already drawn by parliamentary agent, perusing and filling up] statement of proofs for examiner for standing orders, and arranging documents referred to therein, and forwarding same, with letter accompanying, to parliamentary agent ..	1	1	0
	or, If lands and houses are taken by the bill	2	2	0

		£	s.	d.
Jan. 8.	Drawing affidavit in part of proofs on standing orders	0	10	0
	or per folio ..	0	1	4
	This includes instructions or attendance on witness, the documents attached, and the copy.			
	Attending swearing same [*or* attending with witness to be sworn] ..	0	6	8
	Writing to parliamentary agent, forwarding statement of proofs, &c...	—	—	—
„ 9.	Attending you, conferring on threatened opposition. Two hours, at 13*s.* 4*d.* per hour	1	6	8
	Drawing petition of —— in favour of bill—If less than eleven folios ..	0	13	4
	If less than fifteen folios ..	1	0	0
	If more than fifteen folios— per sheet ..	0	13	4
	or per folio ..	0	1	4
„ 11.	Having received copy Lord Chairman's remarks on the bill, perusing and considering same	0 to 1	10 to 1	6 to 0
	If long, charge according to time employed, at 13s. 4d. per hour.			
„ 12.	Perusing letter from parliamentary agent stating that a memorial had been deposited against this bill on standing orders			
„ 14.	Having received copy of the memorial which had been deposited against bill, perusing same. If under twenty folios	0	6	8
	If above, per folio ..	0	0	4

		£	s.	d.
Jan. 14.	Long attendance upon you conferring thereon	0	13	4
	Drawing observations on memorial for parliamentary agent, per folio ..	0	1	4
	Letter to him therewith	—	—	—
	Making copy memorial for use before examiner, per folio	0	0	6
„ 20.	Journey to London, attending before examiner on standing orders, when the proofs having been given; and after argument upon alleged non-compliance, the examiner decided that the standing orders had not been complied with—			
	Time, at per day ..	4	4	0
	Hotel expenses, at per day	1	1	0
	Fares, &c.	(sum paid)		
	No charge is allowed for attendance of a clerk, except for the purpose of being examined as a witness; if he does attend, the charge is from 1l. 1s. to 2l. 2s. a day for time (generally 1l. 11s. 6d.), and hotel expenses and fares actually paid.			
Feb. 4.	Having received copy of examiner's report, perusing same	0	10	6
	Drawing statement for Standing Orders' Committee, stating circumstances in favour of dispensing with the standing orders, and forwarding same to parliamentary agent to settle ..	from 0	13	4
		to 2	2	0
Feb. 15.	Having received letter from parliamentary agent, stating that the Standing			

		£	s.	d.
	Orders' Committee in the Commons had reported that the standing orders ought to be dispensed with, letter to you thereon	0	5	0
Feb. 18.	Having received copy of a petition of ——— against bill, perusing same:			
	If under twenty folios ..	0	6	0
	If above, per folio ..	0	0	4
	Drawing marginal notes on petition for use of counsel, per folio	0	1	4
	Copies of petition for counsel, per folio	0	0	6
	Letter to parliamentary agent therewith	—	—	—
March 7.	Attending Mr. A. on his bringing a clause proposed to be inserted in the bill on behalf of ———, and afterwards perusing same..	0	6	8
„ 14.	Attending you and Mr. A. settling this clause	0	13	4
	Copy of same, per folio	0	0	6
	Letter to parliamentary agent thereon and therewith	0	5	0
„ 16.	Attending you, communicating receipt of letter from parliamentary agent, stating that the bill had passed the Standing Orders' Committee in the Lords	0	6	8
April 8.	Attending you in long conference as to evidence to be given in support of the bill (upwards of an hour) ..	1	1	0

		£	s.	d.
April 8.	Writing Mr. —— of —— for appointment to confer as to evidence he could give in support of bill.. ..	0	3	6
„ 10.	Attending you, conferring on clause 21	0	6	8
	Letter to parliamentary agent thereon	—	—	—
„ 18.	Attending you, conferring on future proceedings	0	13	4
„ 21.	Journey to London to meet Mr. —— and parliamentary agent, and at consultation on opposition, and as to evidence necessary to meet same			
	Time, per day	4	4	0
	Hotel expenses, per day	1	1	0
	Fares, &c.	(sum paid)		
„ 25.	Instructions for brief (according to circumstances).			
	Drawing same, per sheet of ten folios..	0	13	4
	Where documents are copied to form part of the brief, they are not allowed to be charged as drawing, but as copies only, at 6d. per folio.			
	Copies thereof for counsel, not exceeding three .. .. at per folio	0	0	6
	Instructions for proof of Mr. —— ..	0	13	4
	Including attendance on the witness to take notes of his evidence.			
	Drawing proofs, per sheet of ten folios .	0	13	4
	Copies thereof for counsel, not exceeding three	0	0	6

		£ s. d.
May 5.	Journey to London, when bill passed through committee—	
	Time, at per day	4 4 0
	Hotel expenses	1 1 0
	Fares, &c. ..	(sum paid)
	No charge is allowed for the attendance of a clerk, except for the purpose of being examined as a witness; but if the charge is made it should be 1l. 11s. 6d. for time, and the sum actually paid for fares and hotel expenses.	
„ 7.	Perusing and revising amended bill and writing marginal notes (according to time employed, at per hour) ..	0 13 4
	Letter therewith to parliamentary agent	— — —
„ 10.	Letter from parliamentary agent, stating that bill had been before the examiner as to compliance with Lords' Standing Orders not previously inquired into, and that the examiner had certified that none were applicable	— — —
„ 12.	Attending you, conferring on threatened opposition in the Lords	0 13 4
„ 17.	Having received letter from parliamentary agent for information as to evidence to be given before Lords' Committee, attending you thereon	0 13 4
„ 18.	Attending Mr. ——, informing him he would be wanted to give evidence before Lords' Committee	0 6 8

		£	s.	d.
June 1.	Having received copy of petition against, in the Lords, perusing same:			
	If under twenty folios ..	0	6	8
	If above, per folio ..	0	0	4
	Drawing marginal notes on petition for use of counsel, per folio	0	1	4
	Copies of petition for counsel, per folio	0	0	6
	Long and special letter to parliamentary agent thereon, exceeding six folios	0	10	0
„ 3.	Instructions for brief	0	13	4
		and upwards		
	Drawing same, per sheet of ten folios..	0	13	4
	Copies thereof for counsel, viz., one for each, at per folio	0	0	6
„ 6.	Instructions for proof of Mr. —— ..	0	13	4
	Drawing same, per sheet of ten folios..	0	13	4
	Copies thereof for counsel, viz., one for each, at per folio	0	0	6
	See p. 99, for fuller details as to brief, proofs, &c.			
„ 7.	Journey to London, engaged with parliamentary agent arranging as to proofs before Lords' committee, subsequently attending committee when bill passed the committee—			
	Time, at per day	4	4	0
	Hotel expenses, at per day	1	1	0
	Fares, &c.	(sum paid)		
„ 13.	Attending you, conferring on progress made with bill	0	6	8

		£ s. d.
June 15.	Letter to parliamentary agent acknowledging receipt of letter informing me of Royal Assent to Act ..	
	Sessional Fee [see p. 139 for attendances, &c. included in it] ..	10 10 0
	But if the bill does not receive the Royal Assent, then charge 2l. 2s. and upwards, instead of 10l. 10s.	
	£	

Disbursements.

[Here follow all disbursements.*]

£

£

* A charge, taken from the petty cash book, is generally made for postages and incidental expenses.

A LOCAL ATTORNEY'S OR SOLICITOR'S BILL OF COSTS *for promoting a Private Bill of the Second Class under the Standing Orders.*

[See note, p. 92.]

In Parliament,
SESSION 1864.

THE ——— COMPANY, DR.

TO MESSRS. ———, of ———,

Solicitors,

In respect of the Promotion, in Parliament, on behalf of the said Company, of the ——— Act, 1864.

1863.		£	s.	d.
Oct. 7.	Long conference with you on subject of proposed application to parliament for the bill. Two hours, at 13*s.* 4*d.* per hour	1	6	8
„ 8.	Long letter to parliamentary agent, stating the objects of the proposed bill	0	10	0
„ 9.	Attending meeting of directors, conferring and discussing objects of bill, upwards of an hour	1	1	0
„ 12.	Perusing letter received from parliamentary agent advising as to notice for bill	—	—	—

		£	s.	d.
Oct. 12.	Instructions for notice in Gazette and newspapers	0	13	4
	Drawing notice—			
	If less than eleven folios ..	1	1	0
	If more that eleven folios, per folio	0	2	0
	Letter to parliamentary agent therewith	—	—	—
„ 20.	Having received draft notice from parliamentary agent, attending engineer, conferring thereon ..	0	13	4
	Letter to parliamentary agent therewith amended	0	5	0
„ 26.	Having received notice from parliamentary agent finally settled, copy thereof for —— newspaper, at per folio	0	0	6
	Attending newspaper office, or forwarding notice, if at a distance, with instructions	0	6	8
	If a journey to a town where a newspaper is published becomes necessary, the charge is as for a clerk from 1l. 1s. to 2l. 2s. a day for time, and hotel expenses and fares actually paid; but such journies are not justifiable if a letter would answer the purpose.			
Nov. 4.	Examining proofs of notice and ordering insertion for three weeks, or otherwise	0	6	8

			£	s.	d.
		If a revise is necessary, an addition for ordering revise and examining same, of each revise	0	10	0
		No other or further charge is allowed with reference to printing the notice. *The foregoing charges apply to each newspaper, the insertion in the Gazette is done by the parliamentary agent.* *No charge is allowed for copies of the notice for deposit with the plans, &c., printer's slips being so deposited.*			
Nov.	6.	Long attendance on you, conferring ..	0	13	4
„	7.	Examining notice on its insertion in —— newspaper	0	3	4
		Clerks engaged taking reference— For each clerk, at per day, time	1	11	6
		Hotel expenses and fares, &c. ..	(sum actually paid)		
		Examining notice on its insertion in —— newspaper	0	3	4
„	18.	Drawing book of reference, per folio..	0	2	0
		Copies thereof for deposit, as required by Standing Orders, at per folio..	0	0	9
		One copy only is allowed, for the deposit of portions thereof amongst parish clerks.			
		Copy for marking section, for applications to owners, &c., at per folio..	0	0	6
		Copy for use of engineer or other professional person engaged in the			

		£	s.	d.
	case, if positively requisite, at per folio	0	0	4
	Although the book of reference is frequently printed, the copies before stated are allowed as copies, but the printer's bill must not be charged.			
Nov. 21.	Examining notice on its insertion in —— newspaper	0	3	4
„ 30.	Examining and making up plans and books of reference for the purpose of deposit, each set	0	10	6
	The examining and making up the deposits for the parish clerks to be charged according to the time occupied.			
	Attending at office of clerk of the peace, depositing plans, sections and book of reference, &c.	0	13	4
	Attending clerk of the parish of ——, depositing so much of plans, &c. as relate to such parish	0	13	4
	If deposits are made at a distance, or if such deposits are numerous, clerk's time at 1l. 11s. 6d. per day, and hotel expenses and fares actually paid, must be charged. The deposits in London are made by the parliamentary agent.			
	The charge for deposit includes drawing a memorandum of the deposit, and obtaining signature thereto, and the requisite copies thereof, except the same exceed one folio, when 1s. 4d. per folio may be charged for drawing, and 6d. per folio for copies to hand in to examiner, &c.; it also includes the drawing and obtaining the receipt for such deposit.			
	Letter to parliamentary agent, informing him deposits had been made..	—	—	—

		£	s.	d.
Dec. 4.	Instructions for bill	2	2	0
	Drawing bill, at per folio	0	2	0
	Additional clauses are allowed at the same rate.			
	Letter to parliamentary agent therewith	—	—	—
„ 7.	Drawing index to book of reference, and register therewith, for preparing applications and entering up service thereof, with answers received (including necessary copies), per folio	0	1	4
	Drawing a fair copy for service, applications or notices to owners, lessees and occupiers of property, with schedules thereto and letter of assent, dissent or neutrality to accompany same at, each notice ..	0	10	0
	The entering the replies received from time to time is covered by the charge for drawing the lists of owners, &c. for deposit.			
	Drawing list of applications to be posted (or to be served by a clerk), each list	0	3	4
	or per folio ..	0	1	4
	This charge covers a copy for signature and the obtaining the signature of witness thereto, and no second charge is allowed for drawing the lists for handing in to the examiner, or other purpose, but only the charge for copying.			

		£	s.	d.
Dec. 7.	Attending posting applications and taking postmaster's receipt ..	0	13	4

This method of service should always be adopted, if practicable and most economical, the towns however in which applications may, by the standing orders be posted, are limited, and it therefore becomes necessary to forward the applications to an agent at the nearest of such towns, for the purpose of postal.

If personal service is required or a journey is made to a post town, clerk's time and expenses may be charged.

A separate charge for service is not allowed, except under special circumstances.

		£	s.	d.
„ 12.	Letter to parliamentary agent acknowledging receipt of proof of bill, and requesting information as to affidavits of service of applications ..	—	—	—
„ 14.	Journey to London to confer with parliamentary agent on bill, and future proceedings thereon.			
	Time, at 4*l*. 4*s*. per day	16	16	0
	Hotel expenses, at 1*l*. 1*s*. a day ..	4	4	0
	Fares, &c. ..	(sum paid)		

No charge is allowed for "time" on Sundays, but hotel expenses only.

Travelling at night is reckoned as a day.

The time charge covers all work done in the time, and no detailed charges during the period must be made, excepting when done at home by a partner or clerk.

		£	s.	d.
Dec. 16.	Drawing petition for leave to bring in bill—			
	If less than eleven folios ..	1	1	0
	If more, per folio	0	2	0
	Writing parliamentary agent therewith to settle	0	3	6
„ 18.	Having received petition for bill back from parliamentary agent settled, ingrossing same, per folio ..	0	0	9
	Letter to Mr. —— for appointment to sign petition	0	3	6
„ 19.	Attending Mr. —— at his house, procuring his signature to petition for bill	0	13	4
	Attending Mr. ——, who called to sign same	0	6	8
	Letter to parliamentary agent with petition	—	—	—
	Having received letter from Mr. ——'s agent that he intended to oppose the bill, letter to him thereon ..	0	5	0
„ 21.	Journey to —— to see Mr. ——, and discussing the motives of his intended opposition, when we eventually came to terms—engaged half a day	2	2	0
	Fares, &c. ..	(sum paid)		

		£	s.	d.
Dec. 21.	Drawing estimate of expense	0	10	6
	This charge includes the requisite copies.			
	Drawing lists of owners, lessees, and occupiers, for deposit, per folio ..	0	2	0
	Two copies for deposit, per folio ..	0	0	9
	Drawing declaration as to capital, shares, &c...	1	1	0
	This charge includes the requisite copies.			
	Attending Mr. ——, obtaining his signature thereto	0	6	8
	Forwarding these documents to parliamentary agent for deposit ..	—	—	—
„ 31.	Drawing requisition to clerk in Private Bill Office for his warrant for payment of parliamentary deposit ..	0	10	0
	This charge includes copy for signature.			
1864. Jan. 5.	The parliamentary agent having returned the requisition for warrant to receive deposit, attending different promoters for their signature thereto, each..	0	6	8
	Attending the engineer on his arrival, discussing various matters, and particularly opposition of Mr. ——	0	13	4
„ 6.	Letter to engineer requesting him to meet Mr. ——	0	3	6

		£	s.	d.
Jan. 6.	Preparing circulars convening meeting of directors, each	0	1	0
„ 8.	Attending meeting of directors relative to obtaining money for the deposit, upwards of an hour	1	1	0
	Drawing warrant for payment of parliamentary deposit	0	10	0
	This includes copy for signature.			
	Letter to parliamentary agent therewith, and as to money to be deposited	0	5	0
„ 12.	Perusing letter from parliamentary agent stating that a memorial had been deposited against this bill, on standing orders	—	—	—
„ 14.	Having received copy of memorial, perusing same:			
	If under twenty folios ..	0	6	8
	If above, per folio ..	0	0	4
	Long attendance upon you, conferring thereon	0	13	4
„ 16.	Drawing observation on memorial for parliamentary agent—per folio ..	0	1	4
	Letter to him therewith	—	—	—
	Copy memorial, for use before examiner—per folio	0	0	6

		£	s.	d.
Jan. 18.	Drawing [or if already drawn by parliamentary agent, perusing and filling up] statement of proofs for examiner for standing orders, and arranging documents referred to therein, and forwarding same with letter to parliamentary agent	3	3	0
„ 19.	Drawing affidavit by Mr. ——, as to applications to owners, &c., served by him	0	10	0
	Or per folio	0	1	4
	This includes instructions or attendance on witness, list of owners, &c. attached, and copy.			
	Attending, swearing same [or attending with witness to be sworn] ..	0	6	8
	These charges are repeated for each affidavit.			
	Letter to parliamentary agent forwarding statement of proofs, &c. ..	—	—	—
„ 20.	Journey to London, attending before the examiner on standing orders, when proofs having been given; and after argument upon allegations in memorial, the examiner decided that the standing orders had not been complied with—			
	Time, per day	4	4	0
	Hotel expenses, per day	1	1	0
	Fares &c.	(sum paid)		
	No charge is allowed for attendance			

		£	s.	d.
	of a clerk, except for the purpose of being examined as a witness; if he does attend, the charge is from 1l. 1s. to 2l. 2s. a day, for time (generally 1l. 11s. 6d.), and hotel expenses and fares as actually paid.			
Jan. 23.	Attending you, conferring on result of proceedings before examiner ..	0	13	4
„ 25.	Drawing petition in favour of bill—			
	If less than eleven folios	0	13	4
	If less than fifteen folios	1	0	0
	If more than fifteen folios, per folio	0	1	4
	No charge is allowed for instructions for petition, or for endorsing and making up same.			
„ 26.	Engaged amongst local supporters, obtaining their signatures to petition in favour of bill—One whole day	4	4	0
„ 27.	Perusing Lord Chairman's remarks on print of bill sent us by agent, and drawing observations thereon ..	0	10	6
	Or per hour	0	13	4
	Letter to agent therewith	—	—	—
„ 30.	Letter to agent directing him to retain Mr. ——	0	5	0
Feb. 4.	Perusing copy of examiner's report ..	0	10	6
	Drawing statement for Standing Orders' Committee, stating circumstances in favour of dispensing with the standing orders, and forwarding same to parliamentary agent to settle	from 0 to 2	13 0	4 0

		£	s.	d.
Feb. 15.	Having received letter from parliamentary agent, stating that the Standing Orders' Committee in the Commons had reported that the standing orders ought to be dispensed with, letter to you thereon	0	5	0
	Attending engineer in long conference as to evidence necessary to support the bill	0	13	4
	Attending meeting of directors, discussing negotiations with opponents and other matters, engaged two hours	2	2	0
„ 16.	Attending Mr. ———, ascertaining whether he could give evidence in favour of bill	0	13	4
„ 17.	Instructions for proofs of evidence of engineer	0	13	4
	Drawing proofs, per sheet	0	13	4
„ 21.	Journey to —— to obtain evidence in support of bill, attending [*here set out names*], inquiring as to their ability to give such evidence—			
	Time, per day	4	4	0
	Hotel expenses, per day	1	1	0
	Fares	(sum paid).		
„ 22.	Having received copy of a petition of ——— against bill, perusing same:			
	If under twenty folios ..	0	6	8
	If above, per folio ..	0	0	4

		£	s.	d.
Feb. 22.	Drawing marginal notes on petition for use of counsel, per folio	0	1	4
	Copies of petition for counsel, per folio	0	0	6
	Letter to parliamentary agent therewith	—	—	—
March 7.	Attending Mr. A. on his bringing a clause proposed to be inserted in the bill on behalf of ——, and afterwards perusing same ..	0	6	8
„ 14.	Attending you and Mr. A. settling this clause	0	13	4
	Copy of same, per folio	0	0	6
	Letter to parliamentary agent thereon and therewith	0	5	0
„ 16.	Attending you, communicating receipt of letter from parliamentary agent stating that the bill had passed the Standing Orders' Committee in the Lords	0	6	8
April 8.	Attending you in long conference as to evidence to be given in support of the bill (upwards of an hour) ..	1	1	0
	Writing Mr. —— of —— for appointment to confer as to evidence he could give in support of bill ..	0	3	6
„ 10.	Attending you, conferring on clause 21	0	6	8
	Letter to parliamentary agent thereon	—	—	—
„ 18.	Attending you, conferring on future proceedings	0	13	4

		£	s.	d.
April 21.	Journey to London to meet engineer and parliamentary agent, and at consultation on opposition, and as to evidence necessary to meet same. Time, per day	4	4	0
	Hotel expenses, per day	1	1	0
	Fares, &c.	(sum paid)		
„ 25.	Instructions for brief (according to circumstances).			
	Drawing brief, per sheet of ten folios ..	0	13	4
	Where documents are copied to form part of the brief, they are not allowed to be charged as drawing, but as copies only.			
	Copies thereof for counsel, not exceeding three, at per folio	0	0	6
„ 27.	Instructions for proof of Mr. ——, including attendance on the witness to take notes of his evidence ..	0	13	4
	Drawing proofs, per sheet of ten folios .	0	13	4
	Copies thereof for counsel, not exceeding three, at per folio	0	0	6
	And so on for all the proofs; see p. 40, for further details as to briefs, proofs, &c.			
May 5.	Journey to London, attending committee on bill, when bill passed through committee. Time, per day	4	4	0
	Hotel expenses, per day	1	1	0
	Fares, &c.	(sum paid)		
	No charge is allowed for the attendance of a clerk, except for the purpose of being examined as a witness; but if the charge is made it should be 1l. 11s. 6d. for time, and			

		£ s. d.
	the sum actually paid for fares and hotel expenses.	
	If it is found necessary in heavy cases for the second principal of a firm to attend in London, to assist during the promotion or opposition of a bill in the Houses, he is only entitled to charge 2l. 2s. a day for his time and hotel expenses.	
May 10.	Perusing and revising Amended Bill and writing marginal notes, at per hour	0 13 4
„ 12.	Letter therewith to parliamentary agent	— — —
	Letter from parliamentary agent, stating that bill had been before the examiner as to compliance with Lords' Standing Orders not previously inquired into, and that the examiner had certified that none were applicable	— — —
„ 15.	Attending you, conferring on threatened opposition in the Lords	0 13 4
„ 17.	Having received letter from parliamentary agent for information as to evidence to be given before Lords' Committee, attending you thereon	0 13 4
„ 18.	Attending Mr. ——, informing him he would be wanted to give evidence before Lords' Committee	0 6 8
June 1.	Having received copy of petition against, in the Lords, perusing same—	
	If under twenty folios	0 6 8
	If above, per folio ..	0 0 4

		£	s.	d.
June 1.	Drawing marginal notes on petition for use of counsel, per folio	0	1	4
	Copies of petition for counsel, per folio	0	0	6
	Long and special letter to parliamentary agent thereon, exceeding six folios	0	10	0
„ 3.	Instructions for brief			
	Drawing same, per sheet of ten folios..	0	13	4
	Copies thereof for counsel, viz., one for each, at per folio	0	0	6
„ 6.	Instructions for proof of Mr. —— ..	0	13	4
	Drawing same, per sheet of ten folios..	0	13	4
	Copies thereof for counsel, viz., one for each .. .. at per folio	0	0	6
	And so on for all the proofs. See p. 40, for fuller details as to brief, proofs, &c.			
„ 7.	Journey to London, engaged with parliamentary agent arranging as to proofs before Lords' committee, subsequently attending committee when bill passed the Committee—			
	Time, at per day	4	4	0
	Hotel expenses, at per day	1	1	0
	Fares, &c.	(sum paid)		
„ 13.	Attending you conferring on progress made with bill	0	6	8
„ 15.	Letter to parliamentary agent acknowledging receipt of letter informing me of Royal Assent to Act ..	—	—	—

	£	s.	d.
Sessional Fee [see p. 139 for attendances, &c. included in it] ..	10	10	0
But if the bill does not receive the Royal Assent, then charge 2l. 2s. and upwards, instead of 10l. 10s.			
£			

Disbursements.

[Here follow all disbursements.*]

£

£

* A charge, taken from the petty cash book, is generally made for postages and incidental expenses.

CHAPTER II.

COUNSEL.

PREVIOUSLY to Session 1864, the fees for counsel were invariably as follows:—

		£	s.	d.
Retainer		5	5	0
	Clerk	0	10	6
Brief (which does not cover the first day's attendance in committee)		10	10	0 and upwards.
	Clerk	0	10	6
Consultation		5	5	0
	Clerk	0	10	6
Committee .. .. .. (each day)		10	10	0
	Clerk	0	10	6

Great dissatisfaction, however, having for some time existed in regard to the system under which fees were paid to counsel, the subject engaged the attention of the Select Committee of the House of Commons on Private Bill Legislation, which sat in Session 1863, and that Committee, after hearing the evidence of the Attorney-General on the subject, reported against the system as then existing.

A general feeling, however, prevailing, that it would be most advisable that any alterations in their fees should be made by the members of the parliamentary Bar themselves, and an intimation having been conveyed to certain members of the House that the subject was under their consideration, no action was taken by the House in the matter, when they carried out the other recommendations of the committee in the beginning of Session 1864.

The objections to the fees as existing were twofold; 1stly, the high amount of the fees which were paid for retainer and consultation so far exceeding as they did the corresponding fees payable before the Courts of Law and Equity; and secondly, that, according to what was understood to be the etiquette of the Bar, a junior counsel could not accept, in respect of retainer, consultation and refresher, a smaller amount than the high fees which were paid to the leading members of the parliamentary Bar.

The parliamentary Bar have now, as it is understood, abolished all rules which were previously considered as restricting counsel from accepting a lower fee than those above enumerated, and it is now understood that a counsel may accept any fee in Parliament which he might accept in other Courts.

CHAPTER III.

WITNESSES.

The charges and expenses of witnesses on private bills can be taxed by the taxing officer, provided the solicitor or agent puts them into the form of a bill as against his client, and then sets out the particulars of the witnesses' charges below; it is not necessary that the solicitor's or agent's own costs should be brought in for taxation to effect the taxation of witnesses' charges, if the above course be adopted.

*Scale.**

Note.—Sundays are not allowed to be charged as time. Fares are allowed as actually paid.

	Time.			Hotel Expenses. (If from Home.)		
	£	s.	d.	£	s.	d.
Accountants	1	1	0	1	0	0
Apothecaries	1	1	0	1	0	0
Architects	1	1	0	1	1	0
		to				
	2	2	0			
Auctioneers	0	15	0	0	15	0
		to			to	
	1	1	0	1	1	0
Barristers	2	2	0	1	1	0

* The following Scale is that ordinarily allowed, but higher charges are sometimes allowed, under special circumstances, in the case of professional gentlemen.

	Time.			Hotel Expenses. (If from Home.)		
	£	s.	d.	£	s.	d.
Chemists and Druggists	1	1	0	1	1	0
Civil Engineers	2	2	0	1	1	0
This does not apply to professional evidence.						
Clergymen				1	1	0
Clerks	0	10	0	0	10	0
		to			to	
	0	15	0	0	15	0
Farmers or yeomen	0	10	0	0	10	0
		to			to	
	0	15	0	0	15	0
Gentlemen				1	1	0
Innkeepers	0	10	0	0	10	0
		to			to	
	1	0	0	0	15	0
Labourers	0	5	0	0	7	0
Mechanics, &c.	0	7	0	0	7	0
		to			to	
	0	10	0	0	10	0
Officers of Army or Navy	1	1	0	1	1	0
Physicians	2	2	0	1	1	0
Police constable	0	5	0	0	7	0
Police serjeant	0	7	6	0	7	0
		to			to	
Police superintendent	0	15	0	0	10	6
Soldiers, common	0	5	0	0	7	0
Solicitors	1	1	0	1	1	0
		to				
	2	2	0			
Surgeons	2	2	0	1	1	0
Surveyors	1	1	0	1	1	0
Tradesmen	0	7	6	0	7	6
		to			to	
	0	15	0	0	15	0

SECTION III.

CHARGES SANCTIONED BY THE SPEAKER AND THE CLERK OF THE PARLIAMENTS, IN ACCORDANCE WITH THE TAXATION ACTS.

In the following scale of charges the authorized lists of charges are consolidated in their integrity, the only alterations and additions being the necessary verbal adaptations of the lists to one another, and the notes printed in italics; the Bills of Costs given in Section II. have been made out on this scale.

ANY charges included in a bill of costs for proceedings previously to those connected with the preparation of the bill, or the notice or plans for the same, or for other proceedings which are not strictly parliamentary, must be made out according to the scale allowed in courts of law.

I.—ATTENDANCES.

For every attendance hereinafter specified, whenever the same shall be necessary and shall be actually had (but not otherwise), parliamentary agents will be entitled to the charges set down in the first column, and solicitors to the charges set down in the second column of this list.

AT THE HOUSES OF PARLIAMENT.

Stages of Bill in either House. At each of the following proceedings in the Houses upon the petition and bill; viz.:—	Parliamentary Agent.			Attorney or Solicitor.		
	£	s.	d.	£	s.	d.
Promoters:						
Attending to obtain petition for bill from the private bill office, and get the same presented and petition referred to standing orders committee, or bill ordered, or other proceeding thereon	1	1	0	1	1	0*
First reading of the bill	1	1	0	1	1	0
Second reading	1	1	0	1	1	0*
Report	1	1	0		—	
Consideration of report	1	1	0	1	1	0*
Third reading	1	1	0	1	1	0*
Consideration of amendments made by the other House	1	1	0	1	1	0

[*Note.*—The above charges will include the attendances upon lords or members at the Houses, who are to present petitions, or to move any stage of the bill in the House, and the drawing the requisite motions, and also the attendances upon officers of the House in reference to matters connected with any stage of the bill or other proceeding; except under special circumstances.

* When the solicitor is also acting as parliamentary agent, he will be entitled to charge 2*l.* 2*s.* for his attendance at the House on these stages of the bill.

	Parliamentary Agent.			Attorney or Solicitor.		
All other special attendances in reference to other proceedings in the House may be charged according to the circumstances of each case, in conformity with such parts of this list as may be applicable thereto.]	£	s.	d.	£	s.	d.
Examiners:						
Attendances before the *examiners of petitions* for private bills, House of Commons, and of standing orders, House of Lords.						
Unopposed Cases:						
To prove compliance with the standing orders in the case of a petition for a bill, and obtaining indorsement by examiner.						
In first class bills	2	2	0	2	2	0
In second class bills	3	3	0	3	3	0
If adjourned for further proofs, each subsequent attendance when the examiner shall inquire into the same, or attending to apply for postponement or adjournment ..	1	1	0	1	1	0
[*Note.*—Only one attendance is allowed to be charged for proofs before the examiner in respect of the standing orders of both Houses, when the same are taken simultaneously.]						
To prove compliance with the standing orders in the case of bills from the other House, petitions for additional provision, or bills introduced in lieu of other bills which shall have been withdrawn ..	1	1	0	1	1	0

Opposed Cases:	Parliamentary Agent.	Attorney or Solicitor.
	£ s. d.	£ s. d.
For every day on which memorials complaining of non-compliance with the standing orders are inquired into by the examiner (according to circumstances).. ..	from* 3 3 0 to 5 5 0	from 3 3 0 to 5 5 0
For entering appearances upon memorials before the examiner, and watching proceedings in case such memorials are not called on, each day	from* 2 2 0 to 3 3 0	from 2 2 0 to 3 3 0
[*Note.*—When an agent or solicitor appears and attends for two or more memorials, complaining of non-compliance with the standing orders, on behalf of the same clients, against the same bill, he will be entitled to charge one day's attendance only in respect of the same.]		
For every day on which a petition for a bill is on the examiner's daily list, but is not called on	2 2 0	2 2 0
[*Note.*—When two or more petitions for bills, being promoted or opposed by or on behalf of the same clients, are appointed for consideration by the same examiner on the same day, but are not called on, the agents and solicitors of such clients respectively will not be entitled to such charge in respect of each petition for a bill so promoted or opposed, but may charge any sum not exceeding 1*l.* 1*s.* for additional trouble (if any) in respect of each other petition for a bill on the same list; provided that in no case (except under special circumstances) shall a charge exceeding 5*l.* 5*s.* be made in respect of one such day's attendance on behalf of the same clients.]		

* *This does* not *include attending at Private Bill Office taking out appearance.*

	Parliamentary Agent.	Attorney or Solicitor.
	£ s. d.	£ s. d.
For every day on which memorials complaining of non-compliance with the standing orders in the case of bills from the House of Lords, petitions for additional provision, or bills introduced in lieu of other bills, which shall have been withdrawn are inquired into by the examiner	from 2 2 0 to 3 3 0	from 2 2 0 to 3 3 0
Attendances before Committees:		
Attending the standing orders committee of either House each day in which the case is on the list and is heard, postponed, or adjourned ..	2 2 0	2 2 0
Attending the committee of selection, or the general committee on railway and canal bills, House of Commons, when required to attend with reference to the grouping of the bill, or the appointment of the committee, or on other special and necessary occasions	1 1 0	from 1 1 0 to 2 2 0
Committee of either House on the Bill.		
Unopposed Bills:		
Attending when the bill is considered by the committee	from 2 2 0 to 3 3 0	3 3 0
Under special circumstances in railway and other bills	..	from 3 3 0 to 5 5 0

	Parliamentary Agent.			Attorney or Solicitor.		
	£	s.	d.	£	s.	d.
Attending the committee to apply for a postponement or adjournment ..	1	1	0	1	1	0
Opposed Bills:						
Attending the committee every day on which the bill is considered by the committee:—						
When the parties appear without counsel (according to circumstances)	from* 3	3	0	from 3	3	0
	to 5	5	0	to 5	5	0
When the parties appear by counsel and the preamble is considered by the committee	2	2	0*	from 3	3	0
				to 5	5	0
When the clauses of the bill are considered by the committee	from 3	3	0	from 3	3	0
	to 5	5	0	to 5	5	0
[*Note.*—When an agent or solicitor appears and attends for two or more petitions against a bill, on behalf of the same clients, he will be entitled to charge one day's attendance only in respect of the same.]						
Attending to watch proceedings of a committee on a group of bills, when the bill in respect of which the agent or solicitor is concerned stands for consideration, but is not considered by the committee, per day:						
Promoters	2	2	0	2	2	0
Opponents	1	1	0	1	1	0

* *Not including, in the case of opponents, as heretofore, the attendance at the Private Bill Office to take out appearances.*

	Parliamentary Agent.			Attorney or Solicitor.		
	£	s.	d.	£	s.	d.
[*Note.*—In no case (except under special circumstances) must a charge exceeding *5l. 5s.* be made in respect of attending to watch proceedings in the case of petitions against a bill, previously to such petitions being considered.]						
Attending to withdraw a petition ..	from 1	1	0	from 1	1	0
	to 2	2	0	to 2	2	0
[*Note.*—When two or more bills, being promoted or opposed by or on behalf of the same clients, are appointed for consideration by the committee on the same day, but are postponed or adjourned without being considered, or are not separately considered by the committee, the agents or solicitors of such clients respectively will not be entitled to such charge in respect of each bill, so promoted or opposed; but may charge any sum not exceeding 1*l.* 1*s.* for additional trouble (if any) in respect of each other bill so postponed or adjourned, or not separately considered; provided that in no case (except under special circumstances) shall a charge exceeding *5l. 5s.* be made in respect of one such day's attendance upon the committee on behalf of the same clients.] No charge is allowed for attendance of a clerk to the solicitor on a committee, except for the purpose of being examined as a witness.						
Miscellaneous.						
Other Attendances at the House or elsewhere:—						
Special attendances upon the chairman of committees (Lords), Mr. Speaker or the chairman of the committee of ways and means (Commons), in reference to any bill	1	1	0	1	1	0

	Parliamentary Agent.			Attorney or Solicitor.		
	£	s.	d.	£	s.	d.
Attending peers or members at the Houses on special and necessary occasions (other than moving the stages of the bill)	1	1	0	1	1	0
First attendance on chairman of committees (Lords), or Mr. Speaker's counsel to go through bill ..	1	1	0	1	1	0
Subsequent attendances	0	10	6	0	13	4
Special attendances (not included in the sessional fee) upon other officers of the House	0	10	6	0	13	4
[*Note.*—Where more than one of the above attendances at the House take place on the same occasion with reference to the same bill, not more than 1*l.* 1*s.* to be charged for all such attendances unless the time occupied shall exceed one hour.]						
At consultation with counsel ..	1	1	0 when required to attend.	1	1	0
On counsel, at chambers, with retainer; brief; to fix consultation and pay fee; with and for draft bill; and other attendances when fees are paid to counsel		..		0	10	0
Attending at the private bill office to deposit the petition for the bill, with agent's declaration and printed copy of the bill annexed, and other printed copies of the bill, and registering the petition in the general list of petitions	1	1	0		—	
[*Note.*—The making up the petition, with declaration and bill annexed, is included in the above charge.]						

	Parliamentary Agent.			Attorney or Solicitor.		
	£	s.	d.	£	s.	d.
Attending at the private bill office to deposit plan, section and book of reference	1	1	0	1	1	0
Other attendances at the House or offices thereof	0	10	6	0	13	4
Attending to deposit other documents required by the standing orders to be deposited (except bills, amendments, &c., the deposit of which, in certain cases, is included in the sessional fee). *See* II.	0	10	6	0	13	4
If at a distance, and for deposits with parish clerks, &c. (if numerous), clerk's time and expenses are to be charged instead of the preceding.						
[*Note.*—The charge for attending to deposit includes any charge for drawing a memorandum of documents deposited, and obtaining signature of the depositor thereto, and the requisite copies of the same, except the same shall exceed one folio, when 1*s.* 4*d.* per folio may be charged for drawing the same, and 6*d.* per folio for copies to hand in to examiner or other requisite copies; it also includes the drawing and obtaining the certificate or receipt for such deposit.]						
Attendances for the purpose of deposit cannot be charged both by parliamentary agent and solicitor.						
Attending at the private bill office to deposit petitions in favour of or against						

any private bill, and registering the same, viz.:	Parliamentary Agent.			Attorney or Solicitor.		
	£	s.	d.	£	s.	d.
If one petition, or less than three .	0	10	6	0	13	4
If three petitions, and less than seven	1	1	0	1	1	0
If seven petitions, and less than twelve	1	11	6	1	11	6
For any number exceeding twelve	2	2	0	2	2	0
[*Note.*—The endorsing petitions and preparing the same for deposit are included in the above fees, except when the same are prepared by the solicitor, when from 3*s.* 4*d.* to 6*s.* 8*d.* is allowed for endorsing a petition or set of petitions, and transmitting the same to the parliamentary agent for the purpose of deposit (except when included in the sessional fee).]						
On taxing officer, for the purpose of taxation of a bill of costs	from 0	10	6	from 0	13	4
	to 2	2	0	to 2	2	0
[*Note.*—No charge is allowed for copies of a bill of costs for taxation, except when necessarily made for the purpose of depositing the same in the taxing office.]						
On a witness settling his proof (if necessary)	0	6	8	0	6	8
[*Note.*—If attendance requisite on many witnesses on the same occasion, a charge to be made according to time occupied. The attendance on a witness for the purpose of settling an affidavit is included in the charge for drawing affidavit. The attendance on the witness previously to drawing his proof is included in the charge for instructions for proof.]						

	Parliamentary Agent.			Attorney or Solicitor.		
	£	s.	d.	£	s.	d.
With a witness to be sworn	0	6	8	0	6	8
At post office registering and posting applications and taking receipt ..	0	10	6	0	13	4
[*Note.*—The applications to owners, lessees and occupiers should be made by post, if practicable, and more economical. Where personal service is required, a clerk's time and expenses for the purpose of such service may be charged, except where such service can be more economically made through local agents.]						
Preparing and despatching telegraphic message	0	10	0	0	10	0
At private bill office to take out appearances	0	7	6			
[*Note.*—Only one charge to be made for taking out appearances on any number of petitions from the same clients on the same day.]						
On printer with instructions ..	0	6	8	0	6	8
[*Note.*—When attendance to order proofs is charged, no charge is allowed for subsequent attendance to obtain proofs. No attendance to be charged for ordering further additional copies.]						
ATTENDANCES OF A CLERK:						
Before a committee or the examiner to give evidence	0	10	6	0	10	6
If in favour of or against an opposed bill, or in support of, or against allegations of a memorial	1	1	0	1	1	0

	Parliamentary Agent.			Attorney or Solicitor.		
	£	s.	d.	£	s.	d.
To order and obtain copies of a petition or petitions in favour of or against a bill or other documents .	0	7	6	0	6	8
[*Note.*—Only one attendance is allowed to be charged for ordering and obtaining any number of petitions against the same bill at the same time.]						
Other attendances of a clerk	0	7	6	0	6	8

II.—SESSIONAL OR SOLICITATION FEE.

For soliciting the Bill for the Promoters by the Parliamentary Agent.

	£	s.	d.
When the bill has received the royal assent	26	5	0

[In case the bill should not receive the royal assent, a sessional fee of two guineas and upwards may be charged according to the class of bill, and the progress made through its several stages.]

Attendances as follows :—

House of Lords.

Chairman of committees, counsel or secretary:

To deposit bills, clauses and amendments, and afterwards to obtain the same; and all other formal attendances.

Private bill office:

To give notices.

To examine register and other books.

To deposit prints of bills, amended bills and copies of proposed amendments, and also to deliver printed breviates.

Examiners for standing orders:

All formal attendances.

Fee office:

To pay fees, and all other attendances in reference thereto, and with copies of bills when required.

Journal office:

To order and obtain copies of reports, petitions and other papers; except in the case of opposed bills, when 7*s.* 6*d.*

may be charged for attending to bespeak and afterwards to obtain same.

Committee clerks' office:

All ordinary attendances with reference to the progress of the bill.

Bill office:

To deposit copies of bills.

House of Commons.

The sessional fee will include all attendances not otherwise specially mentioned in this list, at the following offices of the House of Commons; viz.:—

At the House for the purpose of watching proceedings, and royal assent.

Chairman of the committee of ways and means:

To deposit bills, clauses and amendments, and afterwards to obtain the same; and all other formal attendances.

Committee of selection or general committee on railway and canal bills:

To deposit bills, and on other occasions when not specially required to attend.

Mr. Speaker's counsel:

To deposit prints of bills, and afterwards to obtain the same; and all other formal attendances.

Mr. Speaker's secretary:

All formal attendances to leave amended bills and clauses, and to obtain the same agreed to.

The examiner:

To deposit bills and apply for appointments; and all formal attendances.

Private bill office:

To give notices.

To examine register with reference to deposit of petitions or memorials against bill, and for other purposes, and other books.

To deposit prints of bills, amended bills, and copies of proposed amendments.

Fee office:

To pay fees and all other attendances in reference thereto, and with copies of bills when required.

Journal office:

To order and obtain copies of reports, petitions and other papers; except in the case of opposed bills, when 7*s*. 6*d*. may be charged for attending to bespeak and afterwards to obtain the same.

Committee clerks' office:

To deposit bills, and all ordinary attendances with reference to the progress of the bill.

Doorkeepers:

To deliver prints of bills, &c.

Offices for the sale of parliamentary papers:

To obtain printed reports and other papers required for use in the progress of the bill.

The sessional fee will also cover all ordinary communications of the agent with the solicitor, with reference to the progress of the bill through its various stages, when no professional advice or instruction is given.

SESSIONAL OR SOLICITATION FEE.

For soliciting the Bill for the Promoters by the Solicitor, when a Parliamentary Agent is also employed.

	£	s.	d.
When the bill has received the royal assent ..	10	10	0

[In case the bill should not receive the royal assent, a sessional fee of two guineas and upwards may be charged according to the class of bill, and the progress made through its several stages.]

The sessional fee of the solicitor will include all charges for his ordinary communications with the parliamentary agent, with reference to the progress of the bill through its various stages, when no professional advice or instruction is given; delivering documents to parliamentary agent for deposit; attendances at the offices of the Houses to ascertain the position of the bill; attendances at the office for sale of parliamentary papers; attendances at the Houses to watch proceedings; and at the royal assent.

When no other parliamentary agent is employed, the solicitor acting in that capacity will be entitled to the sessional fee of parliamentary agent, in lieu of that of solicitor.

In cases of opposition to bills, no sessional fee is allowed.

III.—TIME CHARGES.

	Parliamentary Agent. £	s.	d.	Attorney or Solicitor. £	s.	d.
For attendances, &c.—						
Ordinary	0	10	6	from 0	6	8
				to 0	13	4
If upwards of an hour	1	1	0	1	1	0
Or per hour	0	13	4*	0	13	4*
If required to leave London—						
Time per day †	4	4	0	4	4	0
Hotel expenses	1	1	0	1	1	0
and fares actually paid.						
A solicitor ‡ from the country absent from home in London, or elsewhere, is allowed—						
Time per day †		..		4	4	0
Hotel expenses		..		1	1	0
and fares actually paid.						
[*Note.*—The day charge includes all charges for work done during the day.]						
Clerks: per day†		..		from 1	1	0
				to 2	2	0
Hotel expenses and fares actually paid.						
[*Note.*—In taking the reference, and in serving applications on owners, &c., and making deposits with parish clerks, a charge of 1*l.* 11*s.* 6*d.* per day is allowed for each clerk so employed.]						

* *Where it becomes necessary to assess work done by a principal, by the length of time he is employed, this is the rate, provided the whole charge does not exceed £4: 4s. a day: work done at night is generally allowed at double the day rate.*

† *A time charge is not allowed to be made for Sundays, but only hotel expenses are chargeable.*

‡ *A solicitor attending in London in respect of several bills, on behalf of the same client, must not charge each such bill with the whole time of his attendance, but must apportion the whole time charge as fairly as he can among the several bills.*

IV.—DRAWING DOCUMENTS.

The folio mentioned in the following list means seventy-two words or figures; and the sheet, ten such folios. If, for example, an ordinary brief sheet contains from five to seven folios, the computation of the number of sheets must be made by ascertaining the actual number of folios of seventy-two words in the whole document, and dividing it by ten.

Instructions for drawing documents are only allowed in those cases in which it is specified in the following list; but instructions are not to be charged where the time occupied in getting up the particulars or the perusal of the necessary documents are specifically charged.

In all cases the charge for drawing includes a fair copy for the solicitor's or agent's own use, or for the counsel or an agent to settle.

The charge for a copy includes its examination.

	£	s.	d.
Special instructions (if required), and letters therewith:			
Notice:			
As to contents and publication	1	1	0
Plans:			
As to form and deposit of	1	1	0
Notice to owners, lessees and occupiers:			
As to form and service thereof	0	10	6
Lists of owners, &c.:			
As to form of	0	10	6
[*Note.*—Any other instructions as to the above documents or other requirements of the standing orders to be charged as a letter.]			
Notice in gazette or newspaper:			
Instructions	0	13	4
If less than 11 folios	1	1	0
If more than 11 folios, per folio	0	2	0
Book of reference:			
Per folio	0	2	0
Index to book of reference and register therewith, containing the answers received to applications (including any necessary copies), per folio .. .., ..	0	1	4

	£	s.	d.
Lists of owners, lessees and occupiers:			
Per folio	0	2	0
[*Note.*—The above charges include the entering the replies received from time to time for the purpose of such drawing.]			
Applications to owners, lessees and occupiers of lands and houses:			
Drawing, and fair copy for service, each application (including the letter of assent, dissent or neutrality, left or forwarded therewith)	0	10	0
Each notice of abandonment and other notice not being in the form set forth in Appendix (A.) to the standing orders	0	5	0
List of applications to be posted or to be served by a witness, and copy for signature, including the obtaining the signature of the witness thereto:			
Each list	0	3	4
or, per folio	0	1	4
[*Note.*—No second charge allowed for drawing the above lists of applications for the purpose of handing in to the examiner, or other purpose, but only the charge for copying.]			
Estimates of expense and requisite copies ..	0	10	6
Declaration in lieu or in aid of deposit of money, and requisite copies	1	1	0
Declaration and estimate, and requisite copies ..	1	11	6
Declaration under Standing Order 41, and requisite copies	1	1	0
Subscription contract:			
Instructions	0	13	4
Per folio	0	1	4

	£	s.	d.
Petition for bill:			
If less than 11 folios	1	1	0
If more than 11 folios, per folio	0	2	0
Agent's declaration, and copies for deposit:			
1st class bill	1	1	0
2nd class bill	2	2	0
Bill:			
Instructions	2	2	0
Drawing bill, per folio	0	2	0
Additional clauses, per folio	0	2	0
Statements of proofs on Standing Orders:			
Proofs previously to the introduction of the bill;			
Parliamentary Agent:			
Drawing or perusing same, and fair copy, and forwarding same to solicitor, together with letter accompanying the same, and instructions:			
1st class bill	1	1	0
Ditto, where lands and houses are taken	1	11	6
2nd class bill	2	2	0
Solicitor:			
Drawing or perusing and filling up the same, and arranging lists referred to therein, and forwarding the same, with letter accompanying, to the parliamentary agent:			
1st class bill	1	1	0
Ditto, where lands and houses are taken	2	2	0
2nd class bill	3	3	0

	£	s.	d.
Parliamentary Agent:			
Perusing and finally arranging the same for proof before the examiner:			
1st class bill	0	10	6
2nd class bill	1	1	0
If the solicitor is also acting as parliamentary agent, he may charge for statement of proofs, including final arrangement of the same:			
1st class	2	2	0
Ditto, when lands and houses are taken	3	3	0
2nd class	4	4	0
Proofs subsequent to introduction of bill:			
Solicitor	from 1 to 2	1 to 2	0 to 0
Parliamentary agent	from 1 to 2	1 to 2	0 to 0
Or, if the solicitor is also acting as parliamentary agent	from 2 to 3	2 to 3	0 to 0
No other or further charge is allowed to parliamentary agent or solicitor with reference to the preparation of the statement of proofs.			
Memorials complaining of non-compliance with Standing Orders:			
Instructions	0	13	4

	£	s.	d.
If less than 11 folios	1	1	0
If more than 11 folios, per folio	0	2	0
Statements for Standing Orders' Committee (according to length and other circumstances) ..	from 0 to 2	13 2	4 0
Or, per brief sheet of 10 folios	0	13	4
Petitions against bill, and praying to be heard before the committee:			
Instructions	0	13	4
If less than 11 folios	1	1	0
If more than 11 folios, per folio	0	2	0
Petitions for additional provision, or for dispensing with Standing Orders:			
If less than 11 folios	1	1	0
If more than 11 folios, per folio	0	2	0
Other petitions with reference to bill:			
If less than 11 folios	0	13	4
If less than 15 folios	1	0	0
If more than 15 folios, per sheet	0	13	4
Or, per folio	0	1	4
Briefs:			
Instructions for brief (according to circumstances).			
Drawing same, per brief sheet of ten folios ..	0	13	4

[*Note.*—Documents copied to form part of brief must be charged as copies (*at 6d. per folio*), and not as drawing.]

	£	s.	d.
Retainers to counsel:			
Drawing and copy	0	10	0
Case for opinion of counsel:			
Instructions	0	13	4
Drawing, per sheet	0	13	4
Proofs of witnesses, or notes for cross-examination:			
Instructions (including, in case of proofs of witnesses, any previous attendance on the witness)	0	13	4
Drawing, per sheet	0	13	4
Statements, reports, abstracts, or other documents prepared for use in proceedings of the house, or in preparing to comply with the Standing Orders, per folio	0	1	4
Or, per brief sheet of ten folios	0	13	4
Affidavits (including attendance on the witness):			
Each affidavit, including lists attached thereto, and copy	0	10	0
Or, per folio	0	1	4
Requisition for warrant for deposit of money and copy for signature	0	10	0
Warrant, and attendance to get same signed ..	0	10	0
Requisition for certificate of Speaker	0	10	0
Certificate, and attendance to get same signed ..	0	10	
Requisition for withdrawal of petitions or memorials	0	10	0

	£	s.	d.
Motions, special, for members:			
Drawing and fair copy for member	0	10	0
[*Note.*—Charges for drawing, and copies of all ordinary motions on the several stages of the bills, and other proceedings in the House, to be included in the fees for attendance.]			
Summons for witnesses:			
Drawing, and copy for service	0	5	0
Other documents connected with the case, and not specified above, per folio	0	1	0
[*Note.*—In all cases the charge for drawing any document will include the fair copy to keep, or for counsel or agent to settle.]			

V.—PERUSING, &c.

PARLIAMENTARY AGENTS' CHARGES.

	£ s. d.
For Perusing and Settling Documents drawn by a Solicitor (when required).	
Notices for gazette and newspapers:	
If less than 11 folios	1 1 0
If more than 11 folios (according to length and other circumstances) ..	from 1 1 0 to 2 2 0
Petition for bill:	
If less than 11 folios	1 1 0
If more than 11 folios .. .. .. (Or if the same shall exceed 50 folios, 1*s.* per folio upon the whole petition).	from 1 1 0 to 2 2 0
Petitions for additional provision, or for dispensing with the Standing Orders:	
Petitions against bill, and praying to be heard before the committee, or memorial complaining of non-compliance with the Standing Orders: The same charges as for a petition for a bill.	
Other petitions, against or in favour of bills, each petition	0 6 8

	£ s. d.
Statements for Standing Orders' Committee, reports and other documents (if required), when the same have been drawn by the solicitor (according to circumstances)	from 0 6 8 to 1 1 0
or per brief sheet of ten folios	0 6 8
Perusing and settling bills and preparing the same in parliamentary form and for press:	
For any bill not exceeding 60 folios, according to the length of the bill and the nature and extent of revision	from 2 2 0 to 5 5 0
For any bill exceeding 60 folios, and less than 150, according to the length of the bill, and the nature and extent of revision	from 5 5 0 to 10 10 0
For any bill exceeding 150 folios, according to the length of the bill and the nature and extent of revision; but if above 10*l.* 10*s.*, not exceeding (except under special circumstances) one-half the charge for drawing any such bill..	5 5 0 and upwards.
Perusing and settling clauses and amendments (according to length and other circumstances, but not exceeding 1*s.* per folio).	

[*Note.*—The charges for perusing and settling include a copy as perused and settled for own use, if required, and no copy is to be charged for the purpose of returning the same as settled.

No charge is allowed for perusal and settling by the party who charges for the drawing, but he may charge for a perusal (if necessary) of the document as settled, according to circumstances, but not in any case exceeding half the charge allowed for perusal and settling of the draft.]

PERUSALS.

	£	s.	d.
Perusals, generally, should be charged by the time occupied, but if per folio, not exceeding ..	0	0	4
Obtaining and perusing report of Board of Trade on bill	0	10	6
Perusing a petition or memorial against bill:			
If under 20 folios..	0	6	8
If above, per folio	0	0	4

VI.—COPIES OF DOCUMENTS.

	£	s.	d.
Books of reference, lists of owners, lessees and occupiers, and other similar documents required by the Standing Orders to be deposited:			
For the copies so deposited, when deposited in manuscript,* per folio (of 72 words or figures)	0	0	9
For such copies of other documents as are included in table (A.) annexed, per folio	0	0	6
For ingrossing petitions, memorials, and other parliamentary documents:			
Per folio	0	0	9
For copies of documents not included in table (A.):			
Per folio	0	0	4
[*Note.*—For the number of copies allowed to be charged at 9*d.* and 6*d.* per folio, *vide* table at page 155. In cases where minutes of evidence are printed, copies of the same are not allowed to be charged, but only the cost of printing and the necessary attendances on the printer.]			

* *Books of Reference, although often deposited in print, are allowed for as copies.*

VII.—EXAMINING PRINTED DOCUMENTS.

	£	s.	d.
Prints of bills:			
Proofs	0	13	4
or, per page of print	0	1	0
Revises	0	6	8
or, per page of print	0	0	6
Ordering proofs of estimate or declaration, examining same and all revises, and returning same to printer, with instructions to print	0	13	4
NOTICES IN GAZETTE AND NEWSPAPER:			
Each newspaper:			
Forwarding notice to printer, with instructions ..	0	6	8
Examining proof	0 to 0	3 to 10	4 to 0
Returning proof, and ordering insertion for three weeks, or otherwise	0	6	8
Examining notice on each insertion	0	3	4
If a revise is necessary, an addition for ordering revise and examining same, of each revise	0	10	0
No other or further charge is allowed with reference to printing the notice.			

VIII.—MAKING UP COPIES OF BILLS, AND FILLING UP AMENDMENTS.

	£	s.	d.
Blanking bill, drawing arrangement of sections, and finally settling bill for printer	1	1	0
Making up bill in parliamentary form for House, and deposit of the same	1	1	0
Filling up bills with amendments :			
For the first copy, unless the amendments be very numerous	0	6	8
For each other copy, unless the amendments be very numerous	0	3	4
If new clauses or amendments be added, exceeding six folios, copies of the same may be charged at *6d.* per folio.			
Marking on print of bill the amendments made therein for examiner	0	6	8
[*Note.*—A manuscript copy of the amendments is not allowed to be charged.]			
Altering bill as an act, and attending printer with instructions to strike off copies	0	10	6

IX.—MAKING UP DOCUMENTS.

	£	s.	d.
Examining and making up plans and books of reference for the purpose of deposit, each set ..	0	10	6
Ditto .. Lists of owners, &c., and other documents deposited therewith	0	10	6
The examining and making up the deposits for the parish clerks to be charged according to the time occupied.			

X.—LETTERS.

Letters containing professional advice or instructions	0	5	0
If exceeding six folios in length	0	10	0
Other letters	0	3	6
[*Note.*—The ordinary correspondence between parliamentary agents and solicitors is not to be charged to their clients, but such letters only as contain professional advice and instructions.]			
Circulars	0	1	0

In cases for which no specific charge is stated in the foregoing Table, the charge is to be made out according to the time occupied.

TABLE (A.)

Copies allowed to be charged besides the copy the charge for which is included in that for drawing.

PROMOTERS.	Number of Copies. At 9*d.* per Folio.	Number of Copies. At 6*d.* per Folio.
Notices:		
For *each* gazette and newspaper ..	..	1
Book of reference:		
For *each* deposit of entire book of reference (when deposited in manuscript)	1	
Amongst parish clerks	1	
For marking section for applications	..	1
Lists of owners, lessees and occupiers; for deposit in Parliament	2	
Applications served by a witness; for use before examiner..	..	2
Petition for bill; ingrossed copy for deposit	1	
Bill; for press	..	1
Statements of proofs; for use before examiner:		
For agent	..	1
For solicitor	..	1
For examiner..	..	2
Memorials:		
For agent	..	1
For solicitor	..	1
For engineer (if necessary)	..	1

	Number of Copies.	
	At 9*d.* per Folio.	At 6*d.* per Folio.
Statement for Standing Orders' Committee:		
For committee and use	..	3
Petition against bill:		
For agent	..	1
For solicitor	..	1
For *each* counsel (not exceeding three)	..	1
Briefs:		
For *each* counsel (not exceeding three)	..	1
Proofs of witnesses:		
For *each* counsel (not exceeding three)	..	1
For witness (if required)	..	1
Notes for cross-examination:		
For *each* counsel (not exceeding three)	..	1
OPPONENTS.		
Memorial:		
Ingrossed copy for deposit	1	
For agent	..	1
For solicitor	..	1
For examiner..	..	2
Statement for Standing Orders' Committee:		
For commitee and use	..	3
Petition against:		
Ingrossed copy for deposit	1	
For agent	..	1

	Number of Copies.	
	At 9*d.* per Folio.	At 6*d.* per Folio.
Petition against—*continued.*		
For solicitor	..	1
For *each* counsel (not exceeding three)	..	1
Briefs:		
For *each* counsel (not exceeding three)	..	1
Proofs of witnesses:		
For *each* counsel (not exceeding three)	..	1
For witness (if required)	..	1
Notes for cross-examination:		
For *each* counsel (not exceeding three)	..	1

The copies above enumerated are those ordinarily allowed to be charged. Any further copies of the documents named in the foregoing table, or any copies of documents not named therein, which may be necessary for the case, are to be charged at the rate of 4*d.* per folio.

SECTION IV.

FORMS OF REPORTS AND CERTIFICATES.

Taxing Officer's Report to Speaker.

In pursuance of the "House of Commons Costs Taxation Act, 1847," I do hereby report to the Right Honourable the Speaker of the House of Commons, that, pursuant to the said Act, application has been made to me by
for the taxation of the costs, charges and expenses charged by
[*or* for the taxation of the costs, charges and expenses hereinafter mentioned]
and that, having been attended by
I have accordingly taxed and settled such costs, charges and expenses pursuant to the said Act, and to the "House of Lords Costs Taxation Act, 1849," and that the amount of such costs, charges and expenses has been allowed by me upon and after such taxation at the sum of £
[*or* and that the total amount of such sums so allowed is £].
I further report, that in addition to the before-mentioned sum, I have allowed the sum of £
for costs and fees in respect of this taxation, and I have charged the same against

House of Commons,
June 21st, 1864.

Taxing Officer
of the House of Commons.

SPEAKER'S CERTIFICATE.

In the House of Commons.

Whereas on the 21st day of June, 1864,
esquire, the taxing officer of the House of Commons did report to me, in pursuance of the "House of Commons Costs Taxation Act, 1847," that application had been made to him, pursuant to the said Act, for the taxation of the costs, charges and expenses charged by
solicitor, of for promoting [*or* opposing
on behalf of]
the
Bill, 1864; and that, having been attended by the parties to such taxation, he had accordingly taxed and settled such costs, charges and expenses pursuant to the said Act:

And whereas in such report the said taxing officer did state the amount fairly chargeable in respect of such costs, charges and expenses, together with the costs and fees payable in respect of such taxation:

Now, in further pursuance of the said Act, I do hereby certify that the said costs, charges and expenses were allowed in such report at the sum of £ ,
and that the costs and fees payable in respect of such taxation amounting to the sum of £ ,
were charged by such taxing officer as stated in such report against the .

Given under my hand this twenty-fifth day of July, 1864.

(Signed)

Speaker.

MEMORIAL TO THE SPEAKER.

To the Right Honourable the Speaker of the House of Commons.

The memorial of the undersigned Messrs. , lately acting as solicitors [*or* parliamentary agents] for the Company in their promotion [*or* opposition] to the railway bill in Parliament in the Session of 1864.

Your memorialists beg leave to appeal against the decision of the taxing officer of the House of Commons on the taxation of their bill of costs [*here follows the title of the matter*] adverted to in the annexed report (*a*) of the said taxing officer.

That the appeal of your memorialists against the said taxation and report is on the following grounds:—

1st. That [*here follow the grounds*].

Your memorialists respectfully submit the following reasons for the appeal [*here follow the reasons*].

2nd. That [*and so on as before*].

Your memorialists therefore request that they may, if necessary, adduce evidence in support of their case, and that the said taxation may be amended.

(Signed)

ENDORSEMENT BY THE SPEAKER ON MEMORIAL.

Pursuant to the 10 & 11 Vict. c. 69, s. 9, I do hereby refer this memorial, together with the report, to the taxing officer, and require a further report (*b*) in relation thereto.

(Signed)

10th June, 1864. Speaker.

(*a*) A copy of the report is generally annexed to the memorial.

(*b*) This further report is in the form of a letter, and goes fully into the grounds upon which the charges have been taxed.

TAXING OFFICER'S CERTIFICATE INDORSED ON A BILL OF COSTS TAXED BY HIM ON REFERENCE FROM A MASTER OF ANY COURT.

House of Commons,
1864.

I hereby certify that I have taxed the within costs, charges and expenses, and that the amount thereof, including the costs and fees of taxation, has been allowed by me at the sum of £

(Signed)
Taxing Office of the House of Commons.

Esq.,
Taxing Master, Court of ——.

TAXING OFFICER'S CERTIFICATE ON REFERENCE OF SEVERAL BILLS FROM A MASTER OF ANY COURT.

Whereas
Esquire, one of the taxing masters of her Majesty's Court of has requested me to tax certain bills of costs relating to the
and marked A., B. and C., and indorsed by him with his name:

Now I hereby certify that having been attended by
solicitor for the party charging the said bills of costs [*or*, and due notice of this taxation having been given to the parties concerned in such taxation, and such parties not having attended at same], I have accordingly taxed the said bills of costs, and the amounts thereof have been allowed by me upon and after such taxation at the sums hereinafter specified, viz. [*here follows headings of bills of costs, and amounts allowed*]: and that the total

amount of such sums so allowed is £ ,
and I further certify that I have charged the costs and fees payable in respect of such taxation, amounting to the sum of £ ,
against the parties chargeable with the above-mentioned bills of costs.

Dated 22nd day of February, 1864.

Esq., Taxing Master of the Court of . — Taxing Officer of the House of Commons.

Taxing Officer's Certificate on reference from one of the Judges.

In the Queen's Bench.

The Company of Proprietors of the ,
Plaintiffs.

The Railway Company,
Defendants.

In pursuance of the order of reference of the Honourable Mr. Justice , made in this cause, and dated 14th March instant, I certify that I find that there is due from the Defendants to the Plaintiffs in this action the sum of £

March 26th, 1864. — Taxing Officer of the House of Commons.

Taxing Officer's Certificate on reference from Court of Session.

Skye Water Bill, 1858.

In pursuance of the remit by Lord , Ordinary, in the matter of the petition of , dated the 20th February, 1864, I have, in presence of the parties, taxed the above bill of costs of Messrs. , at the sum of £ , and I also certify that the costs of taxation payable to Messrs. , amount to , such sum being payable by the party chargeable with the said costs; all which I humbly beg to report to the Lord Ordinary.

(Signed)

House of Commons,
February 23rd, 1864.

Taxing Officer
of the House of Commons.

SECTION V.

TAXATION ACTS.

REMARKS ON TAXATION ACTS.

Taxation Acts.

[The only material difference between the taxation acts of the House of Commons and House of Lords is that clauses 10, 11, 12 and 13 of the latter Act are not to be found in the former one; these clauses were the result of the experience arising between the time of the one Act coming into operation and the passing of the other. Clauses 10, 11 and 12 provide for the taxing of the whole of a bill of costs by the officer of either House, although a portion of it may not have been incurred in that House to which the taxing officer who taxes the costs may belong; they also provide for references to the parliamentary taxing officers by officers of other Courts, and for references by the parliamentary taxing officers to such officers of other Courts. Clause 13 empowers the taxing officers to take an account of monies advanced on account.]

---

10 & 11 Vict. c. 69.

An Act for the more effectual Taxation of Costs on Private Bills in the House of Commons.

[22nd July, 1847.]

Whereas an act was passed in the sixth year of the reign of his late majesty King George the Fourth intituled, "An Act to establish a Taxation of Costs on Private Bills in the House of Commons, and to prohibit the Sale of certain Offices under the Serjeant at Arms attending the House of Commons:" And whereas it is expedient to repeal the same, and to make more effectual provision for taxing the costs and expenses to be charged by parliamentary agents, attornies, solicitors and others in future sessions of parliament in respect of bills subject to the payment of fees in parliament, commonly called private bills, and to be incurred in complying with the standing orders of the house of commons relative to such bills, and in preparing, bringing in, and carrying the same through, or in opposing the same in, the house of commons: Be it enacted by the Queen's most excellent majesty, by and with the advice and consent of the lords spiritual and temporal, and commons, in this present parliament assembled, and by the authority of the same, that, except as to any costs, charges and expenses which shall have been incurred in the present or any preceding session of parliament, the said recited act shall be repealed: provided always, that the repeal of the said recited act shall not be construed to revive any act or any provision thereof which was thereby repealed.

6 Geo. 4, c. 123.

Recited Act 6 Geo. 4, c. 123, repealed.

II. And be it enacted, that no parliamentary agent, attorney or solicitor, nor any executor, administrator, or assignee of any parliamentary agent, attorney or solicitor, shall commence or maintain any action or suit for the recovery of any costs, charges or expenses in respect of any proceedings in the house of commons in any future session of parliament relating to any

Parliamentary agent, attorney or solicitor not to sue for costs until one month after delivery of his bill.

petition for a private bill, or private bill, or in respect of complying with the standing orders of the said house relative thereto, or in preparing, bringing in and carrying the same through, or opposing the same in, the house of commons, until the expiration of one month after such parliamentary agent, attorney or solicitor, or executor, administrator or assignee of such parliamentary agent, attorney or solicitor has delivered unto the party to be charged therewith, or sent by post to or left for him at his counting-house, office of business, dwelling-house, or last known place of abode, a bill of such costs, charges and expenses, and which bill shall either be subscribed with the proper hand of such parliamentary agent, attorney or solicitor, or in the case of a partnership by any of the partners, either with his own name or with the name of such partnership, or of the executor, administrator or assignee of such parliamentary agent, attorney or solicitor, or be enclosed in or accompanied by a letter subscribed in like manner referring to such bill: provided always, that it shall not in any case be necessary, in the first instance, for such parliamentary agent, attorney or solicitor, or the executor, administrator or assignee of such parliamentary agent, attorney or solicitor, in proving a compliance with this act to prove the contents of the bill delivered, sent or left by him, but it shall be sufficient to prove that a bill of costs, charges and expenses subscribed in manner aforesaid, or inclosed in or accompanied by such letter as aforesaid, was delivered, sent, or left in manner aforesaid; but nevertheless it shall be competent for the other party to show that the bill so delivered, sent, or left was not such a bill as constituted a *bonâ fide*

Evidence of delivery of bill.

compliance with this act; provided also, that it shall be lawful for any judge of the superior courts of law or equity in England or Ireland, or of the court of session in Scotland, to authorize a parliamentary agent, attorney or solicitor to commence an action or suit for the recovery of his costs, charges and expenses against the party chargeable therewith, although one month has not expired from the delivery of a bill as aforesaid, on proof to the satisfaction of the said judge that there is probable cause for believing that such party is about to quit that part of the United Kingdom in which such judge hath jurisdiction. Power to judge to authorize action before expiration of one month.

III. And be it enacted, that the speaker of the house of commons shall appoint a fit person to be the taxing officer of the house of commons, and every person so appointed shall hold his office during the pleasure of the speaker, and shall execute the duties of his office conformably to such directions as he may from time to time receive from the speaker. Taxing officer to be appointed by the speaker.

IV. And be it enacted, that the speaker may from time to time prepare a list of such charges as it shall appear to him that, after the present session of parliament, parliamentary agents, attornies, solicitors and others may justly make with reference to the several matters comprised in such list; and the several charges therein specified shall be the utmost charges thenceforth to be allowed upon the taxation of any such bill of costs, charges and expenses in respect of the several matters therein specified: provided always that the said taxing officer may allow all fair and reasonable costs, charges and expenses in respect of any matters not included in such list. The speaker to prepare list of charges thenceforth to be allowed.

Taxing officer empowered to examine parties and witnesses on oath.

V. And be it enacted, that for the purpose of any such taxation the said taxing officer may examine upon oath any party to such taxation, and any witnesses who may be examined in relation thereto, and may receive affidavits, sworn before him or before any master or master extraordinary of the high court of chancery, relative to such costs, charges or expenses; and any person who on such examination on oath or in any such affidavit, shall wilfully or corruptly give false evidence, shall be liable to the penalties of wilful and corrupt perjury.

Taxing officer empowered to call for books and papers.

VI. And be it enacted, that the said taxing officer shall be empowered to call for the production of any books or writings in the hands of any party to such taxation relating to the matters of such taxation: provided always, that nothing herein contained shall be construed to authorize such taxing officer to determine the amount of fees which may have been payable to the house of commons in respect of the proceedings upon any private bill.

Taxing officer to take such fees as may be allowed by house of commons.

VII. And be it enacted, that it shall be lawful for the said taxing officer to demand and receive for any such taxation such fees as the house of commons may from time to time by any standing order authorize and direct; and to charge the said fees, and also to award costs of such taxation against either party to such taxation, or in such proportion against each party as he may think fit, and he shall pay and apply

Application of fees.

the fees so received by him in such manner as shall be directed by any such standing order as aforesaid.

On application of party chargeable, or on application of parliamentary agent, attorney or solicitor, the taxing officer to tax the bill.

VIII. And be it enacted, that if any person upon whom any demand shall be made by any parliamentary agent, attorney or solicitor, or executor, administrator or assignee of such parliamentary agent, attorney or solicitor, or other person, for any costs, charges or expenses in respect of any proceedings in the house of commons in any future session of parliament relating to any petition for a private bill, or private bill, or in respect of complying with the standing orders of the said house relative thereto, or in preparing, bringing in or carrying the same through, or in opposing the same in the house of commons, or if any parliamentary agent, attorney or solicitor, or the executor, administrator or assignee of such parliamentary agent, attorney or solicitor, or other person, who shall be aggrieved by the nonpayment of any costs, charges and expenses incurred or charged by him in respect of any such proceedings as aforesaid, shall make application to the said taxing officer at his office for the taxation of such costs, charges and expenses, the said taxing officer, on receiving a true copy of the bill of such costs, charges and expenses which shall have been duly delivered as aforesaid to the party charged therewith, shall in due course proceed to tax and settle the same; and upon every such taxation, if either the parliamentary agent, attorney or solicitor, or the executor, administrator or assignee of such parliamentary agent, attorney or solicitor, or other person, by whom such demand shall be made as aforesaid, or the party charged with such bill of costs, charges and expenses, having due notice, shall refuse or neglect to attend such taxation, the said taxing officer may proceed to tax and settle such bill and demand ex parte; and if pending such taxation any action or other proceeding shall be commenced for the recovery of such bill of costs, charges and expenses, the court or judge before whom the same shall be brought shall stay all proceedings thereon until the amount of such bill shall have been duly certified by the speaker as hereinafter provided: provided always, that no such application shall be entertained by the said taxing officer if made by the party charged with such bill after a verdict shall have been obtained, or a writ of inquiry executed in any action for the recovery of the demand of any such parliamentary agent, attorney or solicitor, or the executor, administrator or assignee of such parliamentary agent, attorney or solicitor, or other person, or after the expiration of six months after such bill shall have been delivered, sent or left as aforesaid: provided also, that if any such application shall be made after the expiration of six months as aforesaid, it shall be lawful for the speaker, if he shall so think fit, on receiving a report of special circumstances from the said taxing officer, to direct such bill to be taxed.

No application to be entertained by taxing officer after verdict obtained.

Taxing officer to report to the speaker.

IX. And be it enacted, that the said taxing officer shall, if required by either party, report his taxation to the speaker, and in such report shall state the amount fairly chargeable in respect of such costs, charges and expenses, together with the amount of costs and fees payable in respect of such taxation as aforesaid; and within twenty-one clear days after any such report shall have been made either party may deposit in the office of the said taxing officer a memorial, addressed to the speaker, complaining of such

If either party complain of report, they may deposit a memorial, and the report or any part thereof, and the speaker may, if he shall so think fit, refer the same, together with such report, to the said taxing officer, and may require a further report in relation thereto, and on receiving such further report may direct the said taxing officer, if necessary, to amend his report; and if no such memorial be deposited as aforesaid, or so soon as the matters complained of in any such memorial shall have been finally disposed of, the speaker shall, upon application made to him, deliver to the party concerned therein, and requiring the same, a certificate of the amount so ascertained, which certificate shall be binding and conclusive on the parties as to the matters comprised in such taxation, and as to the amount of such costs, charges and expenses, and of the costs and fees payable in respect of such taxation, in all proceedings at law or in equity or otherwise; and in any action or other proceeding brought for the recovery of the amount so certified such certificate shall have the effect of a warrant of attorney to confess judgment; and the court in which such action shall be commenced, or any judge thereof, shall, on production of such certificate, order judgment to be entered up for the sum specified in such certificate in like manner as if the defendant in any such action had signed a warrant to confess judgment in such action to that amount: provided always, that if such defendant shall have pleaded that he is not liable to the payment of such costs, charges and expenses, such certificate shall be conclusive only as to the amount thereof which shall be payable by such defendant in case the plaintiff shall in such action recover the same.

Speaker may require a further report.

If no memorial deposited, speaker may issue certificate of the amount found due.

Certificate to have the effect of a warrant to confess judgment.

Construction of certain words in this act.

X. And be it enacted, that in the construction of this act the word "month" shall be taken to mean a calendar month; and every word importing the singular number only shall extend and be applied to several persons, matters or things, as well as one person, matter or thing; and every word importing the plural number shall extend and be applied to one person, matter or thing, as well as several persons, matters or things; and every word importing the masculine gender only shall extend and be applied to a female as well as a male; and the word "person" shall extend to any body politic, corporate or collegiate, municipal, civil or ecclesiastical, aggregate or sole, as well as an individual; and the word "oath" shall include affirmation in the case of Quakers, and any declaration lawfully substituted for an oath in the case of any other person allowed by law to make a declaration instead of taking an oath; unless in any of the cases aforesaid it be otherwise specially provided, or there be something in the subject or context repugnant to such construction.

Form of citing the act.

XI. And be it enacted, that in citing this act in other acts of parliament, and in legal and other instruments, it shall be sufficient to use the expression "The House of Commons Costs Taxation Act, 1847."

Act may be amended, &c.

XII. And be it enacted, that this act may be amended or repealed by any act to be passed in this session of parliament.

12 & 13 Vict. c. 78.

An Act for the more effectual Taxation of Costs on Private Bills in the House of Lords, and to facilitate the Taxation of other Costs on Private Bills in certain Cases. [28th July, 1849.]

Whereas an act was passed in the seventh year of the reign of his late majesty King George the Fourth, intituled "An Act to establish a Taxation of Costs on Private Bills in the House of Lords:" And whereas it is expedient to repeal the same, and to make more effectual provision for taxing the costs and expenses to be charged by parliamentary agents, attornies, solicitors and others, in future sessions of parliament, in respect of bills subject to the payment of fees in parliament, commonly called private bills, and to be incurred in complying with the standing orders of the house of lords relative to such bills, and in preparing, bringing in and carrying the same through, or in opposing the same in, the house of lords, and to facilitate the taxation of other costs incurred in respect of private bills, in certain cases: Be it enacted by the Queen's most excellent majesty, by and with the advice and consent of the lords spiritual and temporal, and commons, in this present parliament assembled, and by the authority of the same, that, except as to any costs, charges and expenses which shall have been incurred in the present or any preceding session of parliament, the said recited act shall be repealed.

7 & 8 Geo. 4, c. 64.

Recited act 7 & 8 Geo. 4, c. 64, repealed.

Parliamentary agent, attorney or solicitor not to sue for costs until one month after delivery of his bill.

II. And be it enacted, that no parliamentary agent, attorney or solicitor, nor any executor, administrator or assignee of any parliamentary agent, attorney or solicitor, shall commence or maintain any action or suit for the recovery of any costs, charges or expenses in respect of any proceedings in the house of lords in any future session of parliament relating to any petition for a private bill, or private bill, or in respect of complying with the standing orders of the said house relative thereto, or in preparing, bringing in and carrying the same through, or opposing the same in, the house of lords, until the expiration of one month after such parliamentary agent, attorney or solicitor, or executor, administrator or assignee of such parliamentary agent, attorney or solicitor, has delivered unto the party to be charged therewith, or sent by post to or left for him at his counting-house, office of business, dwelling-house or last known place of abode, a bill of such costs, charges and expenses, and which bill shall either be subscribed with the proper hand of such parliamentary agent, attorney or solicitor, or in the case of a partnership by any of the partners, either with his own name or with the name of such partnership, or of the executor, administrator or assignee of such parliamentary agent, attorney or solicitor, or be enclosed in or accompanied by a letter subscribed in like manner referring to such bill; provided always, that it shall not in any case be necessary, in the first instance, for such parliamentary agent, attorney or solicitor, or the executor, administrator or assignee of such parliamentary agent, attorney or solicitor, in proving a compliance with this act, to prove the contents of the bill delivered, sent or left by him,

Evidence of delivery of bill.

but it shall be sufficient to prove that a bill of costs, charges and expenses, subscribed in manner aforesaid, or enclosed in or accompanied by such letter as aforesaid, was delivered, sent or left in manner aforesaid; but nevertheless it shall be competent for the other party to show that the bill so delivered, sent or left was not such a bill as constituted a bonâ fide compliance with this act: provided also, that it shall be lawful for any judge of the superior courts of law or equity in England or Ireland, or of the court of session in Scotland, to authorize a parliamentary agent, attorney or solicitor to commence an action or suit for the recovery of his costs, charges and expenses against the party chargeable therewith, although one month has not expired from the delivery of a bill as aforesaid, on proof to the satisfaction of the said judge that there is probable cause for believing that such party is about to quit that part of the United Kingdom in which such judge hath jurisdiction.

Power to judge to authorize action before expiration of one month.

III. And be it enacted, that the clerk of the parliaments, when discharging the duties of his office in person, or in his absence the clerk assistant, shall appoint a fit person to be the taxing officer of the house of lords; and every person so appointed shall hold his office during the pleasure of the clerk of the parliaments or clerk assistant, and shall execute the duties of his office conformably to such directions as he may from time to time receive from the clerk of the parliaments or clerk assistant.

Taxing officer to be appointed by the clerk of parliaments or clerk assistant.

IV. And be it enacted, that the clerk of the parliaments, when discharging the duties of his office in

The clerk of parliaments or clerk assistant to

prepare list of charges thenceforth to be allowed.

person, or in his absence the clerk assistant, may from time to time prepare a list of such charges as it shall appear to him that, after the present session of parliament, parliamentary agents, attornies, solicitors, and others may justly make with reference to the several matters comprised in such list; and the several charges therein specified shall be the utmost charges thenceforth to be allowed upon the taxation of any such bill of costs, charges and expenses in respect of the several matters therein specified: provided always, that the said taxing officer may allow all fair and reasonable costs, charges and expenses in respect of any matters not included in such list.

Taxing officer empowered to examine parties and witnesses on oath.

V. And be it enacted, that for the purpose of any such taxation the said taxing officer may examine upon oath any party to such taxation, and any witnesses who may be examined in relation thereto, and may receive affidavits, sworn before him or before any master or master extraordinary of the high court of chancery, relative to such costs, charges or expenses; and any person who on such examination on oath or in any such affidavit shall wilfully or corruptly give false evidence shall be liable to the penalties of wilful and corrupt perjury.

Taxing officer empowered to call for books and papers.

VI. And be it enacted, that the said taxing officer shall be empowered to call for the production of any books or writings in the hands of any party to such taxation relating to the matters of such taxation.

Taxing officer to take such fees as may be allowed by

VII. And be it enacted, that it shall be lawful for the said taxing officer to demand and receive for any such taxation such fees as the house of lords may from time to time by any order authorize and direct, and to charge the said fees, and also to award costs of such taxation against either party to such taxation, or in such proportion against each party as he may think fit, and he shall pay and apply the fees so received by him in such manner as shall be directed by any such order as aforesaid.

house of lords.

Application of fees.

VIII. And be it enacted, that if any person upon whom any demand shall be made by any parliamentary agent, attorney or solicitor, or executor, administrator or assignee of such parliamentary agent, attorney or solicitor, or other person, for any costs, charges or expenses in respect of any proceedings in the house of lords in any future session of parliament relating to any petition for a private bill, or private bill, or in respect of complying with the standing orders of the said house relative thereto, or in preparing, bringing in, or carrying the same through, or in opposing the same in the house of lords, or if any parliamentary agent, attorney or solicitor, or the executor, administrator or assignee of such parliamentary agent, attorney or solicitor, or other person, who shall be aggrieved by the nonpayment of any costs, charges and expenses incurred or charged by him in respect of any such proceedings as aforesaid, shall make application to the said taxing officer at his office for the taxation of such costs, charges and expenses, the said taxing officer, on receiving a true copy of the bill of such costs, charges and expenses which shall have been duly delivered as aforesaid to the party charged therewith, shall in due course proceed to tax and settle the same; and upon every such taxation, if either the

On application of party chargeable, or on application of parliamentary agent, attorney, or solicitor, the taxing officer to tax the bill.

parliamentary agent, attorney or solicitor, or the executor, administrator or assignee of such parliamentary agent, attorney or solicitor, or other person, by whom such demand shall be made as aforesaid, or the party charged with such bill of costs, charges and expenses, having due notice, shall refuse or neglect to attend such taxation, the said taxing officer may proceed to tax and settle such bill and demand ex parte; and if pending such taxation any action or other proceeding shall be commenced for the recovery of such bill of costs, charges and expenses, the court or judge before whom the same shall be brought shall stay all proceedings thereon until the amount of such bill shall have been duly certified by the clerk of the parliaments or clerk assistant as hereinafter provided: provided always, that no such application shall be entertained by the said taxing officer if made by the party charged with such bill after a verdict shall have been obtained or a writ of inquiry executed in any action for the recovery of the demand of any such parliamentary agent, attorney or solicitor, or the executor, administrator or assignee of such parliamentary agent, attorney or solicitor, or other person, or after the expiration of six months after such bill shall have been delivered, sent, or left as aforesaid: provided also, that if any such application shall be made after the expiration of six months as aforesaid, it shall be lawful for the clerk of the parliaments or clerk assistant aforesaid, if he shall so think fit, on receiving a report of special circumstances from the said taxing officer, to direct such bill to be taxed.

No application to be entertained by taxing officer after verdict obtained.

Taxing officer to report to the

IX. And be it enacted, that the said taxing officer shall report his taxation to the clerk of the parliaments or clerk assistant as aforesaid, and in such report shall state the amount fairly chargeable in respect of such costs, charges, and expenses, together with the amount of costs and fees payable in respect of such taxation as aforesaid, and shall also state in such report the amount due in respect of the said costs, charges, and expenses; and within twenty-one clear days after any such report shall have been made either party may deposit in the office of the clerk of the parliaments a memorial, addressed to the clerk of the parliaments or clerk assistant as aforesaid complaining of such report or any part thereof, and such clerk of the parliaments or clerk assistant as aforesaid may, if he shall so think fit, refer the same, together with such report, to the said taxing officer, and may require a further report in relation thereto, and on receiving such further report may direct the said taxing officer, if necessary, to amend his report; and if no such memorial be deposited as aforesaid, or so soon as the matters complained of in any such memorial shall have been finally disposed of, such clerk of the parliaments or clerk assistant as aforesaid shall, upon application made to him, deliver to the party concerned therein, and requiring the same, a certificate of the amount so ascertained, which certificate shall be binding and conclusive on the parties as to the matters comprised in such taxation, and as to the amount of such costs, charges, and expenses, and the amount due in respect of the same, and of the costs and fees payable in respect of such taxation, in all proceedings at law or in equity or otherwise; and in any action or other proceeding brought for the recovery of the amount so certified to be due such certificate shall

clerk of the parliaments.

If either party complain of report, they may deposit a memorial, and the clerk of the parliaments may require a further report.

If no memorial deposited, clerk of the parliaments may issue certificate of the amount found due.

Certificate to have the effect of a warrant to confess judgment.

have the effect of a warrant of attorney to confess judgment; and the court in which such action shall be commenced, or any judge thereof, shall, on production of such certificate, order judgment to be entered up for the sum specified in such certificate, in like manner as if the defendant in any such action had signed a warrant to confess judgment in such action to that amount: provided always, that if such defendant shall have pleaded that he is not liable to the payment of such costs, charges, and expenses, such certificate shall be conclusive only as to the amount thereof which shall be payable by such defendant in case the plaintiff shall in such action recover the same.

Taxing officer of either house may tax costs not otherwise taxable under the act by virtue of which any bill shall be taxed; and may request other officers to assist him.

X. And be it enacted, that if any bill of costs taxable by virtue of this act, or of "The House of Commons Costs Taxation Act, 1847," shall comprise any costs, charges, and expenses incurred in respect of a private bill, but not taxable by virtue of the act in pursuance whereof such bill shall come to be taxed, it shall be lawful for the taxing officer of the house of lords, or for the taxing officer of the house of commons, as the case may be, either to tax and settle such last-mentioned costs, charges and expenses, or to request the taxing officer of the other house of parliament, or the proper officer of any other court having such an officer, to assist him in taxing and settling any part of such bill; and such officer so requested shall thereupon proceed to tax and settle the same, and shall return the same, with his opinion thereupon, to the officer who shall have so requested him to tax and settle the same; and in taxing such costs, charges, and

Such officers

expenses the taxing officer of the house of lords and the taxing officer of the house of commons respectively shall have the same powers and may receive the same fees in respect of such taxation as if such costs, charges, and expenses were taxable by virtue of this act, or of the "House of Commons Costs Taxation Act, 1847," as the case may be; and the proper officer of any court so requested to tax the same shall have the same powers and may receive the same fees as upon a reference from the court of which he is such officer. to have the same powers as in taxing other costs.

XI. And be it enacted, that the taxing officer of the house of lords, or the taxing officer of the house of commons, as the case may be, may include the amount of such last-mentioned costs, charges and expenses in the report of his taxation of any such bill of costs; and in case the clerk of the parliaments or clerk assistant, or the speaker of the house of commons, as the case may be, shall deliver a certificate of the amount so ascertained and declared in such report, including such last-mentioned costs, charges, and expenses, such certificate shall have the same force and effect as if the whole of such bill of costs were taxable by virtue of the act in pursuance whereof such certificate shall be so delivered. Taxing officers to include certain costs in their reports, and certificates of the amount to be delivered.

XII. And be it enacted, that in case the taxing officer of the house of lords, or the taxing officer of the house of commons, shall be requested by the proper officer of any other court to assist him in taxing and settling any costs, charges, and expenses incurred in respect of a private bill, being part of any bill of costs which shall have been referred to him by the Officers of other courts may request the taxing officer of either house to tax parts of bills.

court of which he is such officer, such taxing officer so requested shall thereupon proceed to tax and settle the same, and shall return the same, with his opinion thereupon, to the officer who shall have so requested him to tax and settle the same, and shall have the same powers and may receive the same fees in respect of such taxation as if application had been made to him for the taxation thereof in pursuance of this act, or of the "House of Commons Costs Taxation Act, 1847," as the case may be.

Taxing officer of either house may take an account between the parties.

XIII. And be it enacted, that it shall be lawful for the taxing officer of the house of lords and for the taxing officer of the house of commons to take an account between the parties to any taxation under this act or the "House of Commons Costs Taxation Act, 1847," of all sums of money paid or received in respect of any bill of costs which is the subject of such taxation, or any matters contained therein, and to report the amount of all such sums of money and the amount due in respect of such bills of costs.

Construction of certain words in this act.

XIV. And be it enacted, that in the construction of this act the word "month" shall be taken to mean a calendar month; and every word importing the singular number only shall extend and be applied to several persons, matters or things, as well as one person, matter or thing; and every word importing the plural number shall extend and be applied to one person, matter or thing, as well as several persons, matters or things; and every word importing the masculine gender only shall extend and be applied to a female as well as a male; and the word "person" shall extend to any body politic, corporate, or collegiate, municipal, civil, or ecclesiastical, aggregate or sole, as well as an individual; and the word "oath" shall include affirmation in the case of Quakers, and any declaration lawfully substituted for an oath in the case of any other person allowed by law to make a declaration instead of taking an oath; unless in any of the cases aforesaid it be otherwise specially provided, or there be something in the subject or context repugnant to such construction.

XV. And be it enacted, that in citing this act in other acts of parliament, and in legal and other instruments, it shall be sufficient to use the expression "The House of Lords Costs Taxation Act, 1849." Form of citing the act.

XVI. And be it enacted, that this act may be amended or repealed by any act to be passed in this session of parliament. Act may be amended, &c.

PART II.

COSTS RELATIVE TO THE TRIAL OF ELECTION PETITIONS.

Remarks.

The law as to costs on trial of election petitions is so fully and ably treated in Rogers' Law and Practice of Elections that it seems right at once to refer the reader to that work; as that work does not deal, however, with any rate of costs, it is necessary to explain that virtually there is no authorized scale of such costs.

The scale usually adopted is analogous to that applied to costs on private bills.

Costs and expenses adjudged by any election committee to be paid, or which become payable under the provisions of the Election Petitions Act, 1848, are taxable under the said act on application being made to the Speaker not later than three calendar months after the determination of the merits of an election petition, or after any order of the House for discharging the order of reference of a petition, or after the withdrawal of any petition; and the Speaker is empowered to refer the same to the examiner of recognizances, or the taxing officer of the House of Commons, for taxation.

ATTENDANCES.

	Parliamentary or Election Agent.			Solicitor.		
	£	s.	d.	£	s.	d.
Ordinary	0	10	6	0 6 8 to 0 13 4		
If upwards of an hour	1	1	0	1	1	0
Or per hour		..		0	13	4
On counsel with papers, &c.	0	10	0	0	10	0
At consultation with counsel	1	1	0	1	1	0
Preparing and despatching telegraphic message	0	10	0	0	10	0
Serving Speaker's warrant on witness, each service		..		0	5	0
Serving notice to attend committee on a certain day, each service		..		0	5	0
But if the persons served with warrants or notices are numerous, and residing close together, clerk's time at 1*l.* 11*s.* 6*d.* per day must be charged in lieu of a charge for each service; and, on the other hand, if the service occupies an unusual time on account of the distance, a charge of 6*s.* 8*d.* or 10*s.* may be made in lieu of 5*s.*; but if a witness lives away at a distance, the warrant or notice may be served through a local agent in the same manner as a subpœna.						

Attendances at House of Commons.

Examiner of Recognizances.

	Parliamentary or Election Agent. £	s.	d.	Solicitor. £	s.	d.
On examiner of recognizances entering into recognizance and procuring indorsement of petition	1	1	0	1	1	0
When objection to recognizances are argued	2	2	0	2	2	0
		to			to	
	3	3	0	3	3	0
Other attendances to peruse recognizance, to lodge objections, &c... ..	0	10	6	0	13	4

House.

	£	s.	d.	£	s.	d.
At House when petition presented .. This fee is only allowed to the solicitor or agent for the petitioner.	1	1	0	1	1	0

General Committee of Elections.

	£	s.	d.	£	s.	d.
On clerk to committee delivering in list of voters to be objected to, or on other matters	0	10	6		..	
When committee determine to strike committee on a certain day, or committee is actually struck	1	1	0	1	1	0
		to			to	
	2	2	0	2	2	0

Committee appointed to try the Petition.

	£	s.	d.	£	s.	d.
Each day the trial is proceeded with ..	3	3	0	3	3	0
		to			to	
	5	5	0	5	5	0
Each other occasion	2	2	0	2	2	0
		to			to	
	3	3	0	3	3	0

TIME.

Solicitors.

A PRINCIPAL is allowed 3*l.* 3*s.*, for an ordinary day's work, but if he is occupied beyond his usual hours, he may charge 1*l.* 1*s.* or 2*l.* 2*s.* more, according to circumstances;* if he resides commonly in the country and comes to London in connection with the trial of a petition, he is allowed 4*l.* 4*s.* a day for time, 1*l.* 1*s.* for hotel expenses, and the sum actually paid for fares.

Parliamentary or Election Agents.

Principals are entitled to 5*l.* 5*s.* for a day's work, but if they go into the country, this sum covers their hotel expenses.

Clerks.	£	*s.*	*d.*
Time, per day	1	1	0
		to	
	2	2	0
Hotel expenses, where necessary	(sum paid)		

DRAWING AND COPIES.

A folio is 72 words, and a sheet 10 folios.

The charge for drawing includes a copy for use or to settle.

Election Petition.		£	*s.*	*d.*
Instructions		0	13	4
Drawing	per folio	0	2	0
Ingrossing	„	0	0	9

* Where the whole of a night is occupied, it has usually been allowed as two days.

		£	s.	d.
Recognizances.				
Drawing	each	0	13	4
Copy	„	0	6	8
Affidavits.				
Instructions		0	6	8
Drawing and copy	each	0	10	0
Objections to Recognizance.				
Drawing and copy	each	0	13	4
or				
Drawing	per folio	0	2	0
Copy	„	0	0	6
Speaker's warrants	each	0	10	0

This is irrespective of the number of names in the warrant, and includes præcipe, drawing, copy for signature, copy for service and attending procuring Speaker's signature.

There is no precise rule as to the number of witnesses to be included in each warrant, where they are numerous, but the number so included should not be less than three or more than six.

		£	s.	d.
Notice to Witnesses to attend Committee on a certain day.				
Drawing and copy for service	each	0	5	0
Lists of Voters objected to, and Bribery and Treating Lists.				
Drawing	per folio	0	2	0
Copies for committee	„	0	0	9
Other copies	„	0	0	6
Brief.				
Instructions (according to circumstances).				
Drawing	per sheet	0	13	4
Copy	„	0	5	0

	£	s.	d.
Proofs of Witnesses; Hints for cross-examination; Statements and other Documents required for use in Committee.			
Drawing .. .. per sheet	0	13	4
Copy .. .. ,,	0	5	0
Retainers to Counsel.			
Drawing and copy .. .. .. each	0	10	0
Notice of withdrawal of Petition, addressed to the Speaker.			
Drawing and copy .. .. .. each	0	6	8
Attested copies and examined copies produced as evidence .. .. per folio	0	0	9

Other documents not mentioned in the foregoing list, and being required in the parliamentary proceeding:			
Drawing .. .. per folio	0	1	4
Copy .. .. ,,	0	0	6
But, if not strictly parliamentary, such as private agreements, &c. and not in any way required in the parliamentary proceeding:			
Drawing .. .. per folio	0	1	0
Copy .. .. ,,	0	0	4

Evidence.

A principal occupied in making enquiries and collecting evidence, whether in support of a petition or to rebut the allegations contained in a petition, is allowed 3*l.* 3*s.* per day.

A sub-agent employed in a similar manner is allowed from 1*l.* 11*s.* 6*d.* to 2*l.* 2*s.*, and clerks from 1*l.* 1*s.* to 2*l.* 2*s.* per day.

Separate charges for attendances on each person from whom information is sought are not allowed in such a number as to exceed in amount in one and the same day the allowance for a day so employed, as stated above.

Perusals.

	£	*s.*	*d.*
If less than 10 folios	0	6	8
to			
	0	13	4
If more,			
Per folio	0	0	4
or			
Per hour occupied	0	13	4

Correspondence.

	£	*s.*	*d.*
Letters containing professional advice or instructions .. ..each	0	5	0
If exceeding six folios in length ..each	0	10	0
Other letters	0	3	6
Circulars	0	1	0

COUNSEL.

The fees to counsel are subject to the same rules as apply to committees on private bills. *Vide* p. 120.

WITNESSES.

The scale of allowances for witnesses is the same as at page 122.

The charges of witnesses are generally settled by the examiner of recognizances on application made at his office.

PART III.

COSTS RELATIVE TO APPEAL CAUSES IN THE HOUSE OF LORDS.

SECTION I.

REMARKS.

THESE costs are taxed at the House of Lords, by the Counsel to the Lord Chairman or his Secretary.

COSTS ALLOWED.	£	s.	d.
Solicitor's retaining fee	2	2	0
Instructions for answer	0	13	4
Drawing and ingrossing same	1	1	0
Paid (parchment)	0	5	0
Instructions for petition for time to lodge cases or for leave to deposit a joint Appendix	0	13	4
Drawing and ingrossing ditto	1	1	0
Instructions for case	2	2	0
Drawing same, 2*s.* per folio of 72 words.			
Drawing Appendix, 1*s.* per folio.			
Copies of documents, 8*d.* per folio.			
Attending consultations with counsel	2	2	0

		£	s.	d.
Attending appeal committee		2	2	0
Attending House on the hearing, per diem.. ..		5	5	0
Attending House when judgment is given		3	3	0
Ordinary attendances		0	13	4
Sessions fee		5	5	0
Letters, messengers and coach hire		3	3	0

COUNSEL.

The following fees are paid to Counsel on Appeal Causes and Causes in Error :—

Retainer		2	2	0
	Clerk	0	5	0
To settle and sign petition		2	2	0
	Clerk	0	5	0
To settle and sign case	from	5	5	0
	Clerk	0	10	6
Consultations		5	5	0
	Clerk	0	10	6

Brief (according to circumstances).

The brief fee covers the first day's attendance.

Refresher		10	10	0
	Clerk	0	10	6

INDEX.

A.

D.

E.

F.

G.

H.

I.

J.

L.

M.

N.

O.

P.

R.

S.

T.

CPSIA information can be obtained
at www.ICGtesting.com
Printed in the USA
LVHW100515130422
716029LV00002B/126

9 783752 594515